NOTES FROM THE GINZA SHIHODO STATIONERY SHOP

Kenji Ueda is a Japanese novelist known for blending fantasy with the charm of everyday life. Born in Tokyo in 1969, he made his debut as a writer in 2021 with *Teppan* (The Iron Griddle), the revised version of a work he wrote in 2019 for the 1st Japan Delicious Fiction Award.

Letters from the Ginza Shihodo Stationery Shop was first published in the UK in 2024. *Notes from the Ginza Shihodo Stationery Shop* is the second volume in the series.

NOTES FROM THE GINZA SHIHODO STATIONERY SHOP

KENJI UEDA

Translated by Emily Balistrieri

MANILLA PRESS

First published in the UK in 2025 by
MANILLA PRESS
An imprint of Bonnier Books UK
5th Floor, HYLO, 103–105 Bunhill Row,
London, EC1Y 8LZ

Originally published as 銀座「四宝堂」文房具店 2 in Japan in 2023
by Shogakukan Inc.

English translation rights arranged with SHOGAKUKAN, Inc. through Emily Books Agency
LTD. and Casanovas & Lynch Literary Agency S.L.U.

Copyright © by Kenji Ueda, 2025
English Translation Copyright © by Emily Balistrieri, 2025
Translated from Japanese by Emily Balistrieri

Quote on page 50 from Nakahara Chūya, *Angel at the Earth's Extreme*, trans.
Jeffrey Angles Copyright © Penguin, May 2026

All rights reserved. No part of this publication may be reproduced, stored or transmitted
in any form by any means, electronic, mechanical, photocopying or otherwise, without
the prior written permission of the publisher.

The right of Kenji Ueda to be identified as Author of this work has been asserted by him
in accordance with the Copyright, Designs and Patents Act, 1988.

This is a work of fiction. Names, places, events and incidents are either the products of
the author's imagination or used fictitiously. Any resemblance to actual persons, living or
dead, or actual events is purely coincidental.

A CIP catalogue record for this book is available from the British Library.

ISBN: 978-1-78658-467-0

Also available as an ebook and an audiobook

1 3 5 7 9 10 8 6 4 2

Typeset by Envy Design Ltd
Printed and bound in Great Britain by Clays Ltd, Elcograf S.p.A.

The authorised representative in the EEA is
Bonnier Books UK (Ireland) Limited.
Registered office address: Floor 3, Block 3, Miesian Plaza,
Dublin 2, D02 Y754, Ireland
compliance@bonnierbooks.ie

www.bonnierbooks.co.uk

Contents

Flash Card Deck   1

Scissors   49

Business Cards   93

Bookmark   141

Coloured Pencils   185

Flash Card Deck

'I got invited to put a book out.' My wife said this just as we started eating dinner.

'Oh, huh.' The tone of my own voice surprised me. *Couldn't I be a bit happier for her?*

'An editor who read the article I published in the city's PR magazine asked if I would write something on food education.'

I guess she didn't find it as cold of a reaction as I did. Maybe it didn't bother her because all I usually replied was, 'Yeah,' or 'Mm-hmm.' I sighed internally.

My wife had long worked at a daycare as a dietician and cook, and for the past few years she'd been an enthusiastic member of the mayor's School Lunch Reform Committee. Apparently there were also people asking her in all earnestness to run for the city council.

Meanwhile, I'd hit retirement age for executive positions at the transportation company I worked for and was currently in a 'supervisory' role, offering advice on safety management. Previously I'd led a large number of staff members with a big budget and extensive authority, and letting go of all of that had been hard.

Here I was sad that my career seemed to be dimming, while my wife's seemed to shine brighter with every year she aged. And discovering that I couldn't be genuinely happy for her was a terrible shock. I felt like such a small man.

Notes from the Ginza Shihodo Stationery Shop

'And this is rather sudden, but apparently this editor will come out from Tokyo to see me, said we could grab dinner and discuss plans for the book. So I don't mean to leave you in the lurch, but please eat out somewhere tomorrow.'

'OK, got it.'

Is this editor a woman? The words were nearly out of my mouth, but I swallowed them. An old man's jealousy is only ever pathetic.

'Thanks for dinner. I'll hop in the bath ahead of you.' With that, I left the table.

I performed a cursory scrub and heaved a sigh without really meaning to the moment I sank into the tub. The thought of the Tokyo trip we had planned for the next week was depressing. *Can we really go with things as they are? As long as we don't end up in a fight that ruins all our plans* . . . Those were the thoughts on my distracted mind.

'Oh, is that it?'

There was a postbox near where my wife was pointing up ahead. It was a rare cylindrical shape you didn't see much these days, and, contrasting with the willow trees swaying in the wind, it was painted a beautiful vermilion.

I opened the map we'd been given at the *yoshoku* restaurant to confirm the shop's location.

'I think so. I guess it's called "Shihodo".'

As we approached, the stone exterior exuded the dignity of a venerable Ginza establishment.

'Somehow it's very Ginza, huh? Do you think it's OK for first-timers like us to go in without an introduction?' My wife sounded worried.

Flash Card Deck

'Hmm. But it *was* Kotomi who told us to come here...'

A short stoop faced the street, and behind that awaited a set of glass double doors. The large doors were decorated – and reinforced at the same time – with well-polished brass that shone with a dull gleam. The glass could have almost been mistaken as mirrors, and in the middle of each door, it said 'Shihodo' in gold letters.

'Hey, my face isn't red, is it?' I asked my wife as I looked at my reflection in the door.

'Well, a little, but not as red as that postbox, so you're fine.'

We'd split just a single bottle of beer at the restaurant, but it was my first time drinking during the day on a weekday, and the alcohol seemed to have caught up with me. No, perhaps I was just intoxicated by the atmosphere in Ginza, seeing as it was my first time having a leisurely visit.

When I pushed the door open and stepped inside, I was immediately enveloped in a pleasant fragrance. I think it was incense, but I couldn't say what scent. Regardless, it was refreshing, like being in a forest.

The shop's ceiling was high, and the sun streaming through the large windows facing the street reflected on the white walls, making it very bright. Wooden display shelves were positioned just the right distance from each other, with all sorts of products neatly arranged on them. It was the kind of shop where even someone like me, who has never been very particular about writing materials, would want to take my time browsing.

'*Irasshaimase.*' Someone must have noticed us standing stock-still a step inside the door because a voice called out from the back. It was a firm voice, well projected, yet with nothing pushy or hurrying about it. It had the warmth of a greeting from the younger brother of a friend whose home you'd gone to visit.

'Hello.' My wife bowed slightly. What's amazing about her is that she's never timid.

'You're Chida-sama, yes? I've been expecting you.'

The man who emerged gave us a deep bow. His outfit was totally normal: light blue shirt, navy tie, grey slacks, black leather shoes with laces; but somehow – whether because the materials were high quality or because the outfit was so well-balanced – he looked ever so elegant.

'Ken Takarada, the manager of Shihodo Stationery, at your service.' I hadn't even seen him take them out, but he was suddenly handing me a business card. One look was enough to tell they were made from quality *washi*. Perhaps the printing type itself was a little old? The typeface had a lot of character.

'I'm Chida. Sorry, I don't have cards with me today.' I apologised, but Takarada-san shook his head.

'Please don't give it another thought. We actually have an old press in the basement. It hadn't been used in ages, but I managed to get connected with someone who could give it an overhaul, so now it works again. I'm just so thrilled about it that I'm handing these out to everyone I meet.'

As he spoke, he handed one to my wife. I was surprised to see her take a card holder out of her purse.

'I'm Miho Chida, though these cards are for work, where I use my maiden name.'

'You even carry those on your days off?'

'I mean, whenever I find an interesting food item, I have to exchange contact info on the spot. I always keep my cards in my bag for that reason.'

Flash Card Deck

Ah, so that's one thing that makes us different, I thought. Though my current business cards were so embarrassing, I couldn't give them out anyway.

'. . . So, our daughter told us to come by,' I said as I put Takarada-san's card in my pocket.

'Yes, she left something with me for you. Right this way, please.'

Takarada-san led us to the back of the shop. The way he carried himself was so flowing and graceful, he reminded me of the leading actor in the *kabuki* performance we had seen the previous day.

At the back of the shop was the till counter, and Takarada-san opened a drawer to remove an envelope. It was the same kind of little envelope we'd received numerous times since arriving in Tokyo.

'This is what she left for you.'

I accepted the envelope. Then Takarada-san took out a pair of scissors.

'Feel free to use these, if you like.'

Thanking him, I cut open the envelope to find a business card-sized flash card inside.

'Another flash card . . .' I turned to look at my wife.

'As expected. What does it say?'

When I wordlessly handed it to her, she took her reading glasses out of the inner pocket of her jacket.

How was lunch? I hope you liked it . . . Salad, consommé, breaded shrimp and Hayashi rice. It's just the usual yoshoku *fare, but don't you think it tastes a little different somehow? The first time I went, I was astounded.*

Notes from the Ginza Shihodo Stationery Shop

'That's true . . .' I found myself murmuring, and my wife nodded emphatically.

'It really is different. Actually, the seasoning was on the light side, and overall, the meal didn't weigh heavily, but there was still a depth to it. It went down so easily but was also so satisfying.'

Since my wife works with food, her comments were apt.

'Yeah, and it smelled different too.'

There was one more card in the envelope.

Shihodo is one of my absolute favourite stationery shops. They do workshops, like for printmaking or seal-carving, on the first floor, but I rented it out for today. Please go on up. I'll tell you what's next up there.

Both cards were written very neatly.

'This ink seems special somehow, too.'

'Yeah, sort of a greyish navy. Not a colour you see every day.'

'But wow, between yesterday and today how many cards is this from her now? All with different-coloured ink.'

'Right. Not only the colours, but each ink seems to flow and soak into the paper in a slightly different way, too.'

I thrust a hand into my jacket's pocket to retrieve the flash card deck on its ring. The cover of the deck had a leathery feel, and the ring itself had been processed to suggest it was made of brass.

As I flipped through, Takarada-san smiled kindly and said, 'They're all lovely colours. So, your daughter has been attending the ink-blending workshops we've been holding on the first floor. Each of the inks on those cards she blended specifically for those messages.'

Flash Card Deck

'Interesting . . .' *When did she get into that?* I wondered. 'Did you know about that?'

'No, it's news to me. But when she gets hooked on something, she really gets hooked, so it sounds like something she'd do. Come to think of it, I seem to remember hearing that she bought some different sort of pen, made of glass, maybe?' My wife took the flash card deck from my hand and flipped through it as she answered.

'I see. The inks are fancy, but so is the flash card deck,' I said.

Takarada-san nodded emphatically. 'The deck is made by a company called Raymay Fujii, a product they simply call "Card Memo". The idea was a flash card deck that adults could feel comfortable using. That leathery cover is special paper made with latex as an ingredient; it's very durable, as it's difficult to bend and highly water-resistant. Your daughter actually came here to buy that as well. Recently, it seems they may be reducing production – I don't get many in these days, and I was worried I might not be able to get one for her in time.'

'Oh dear, what a lot of trouble you've gone to on our account. Thank you so much.' My wife bowed deeply.

'Not at all. I'm grateful to your daughter for her patronage. I should really be the one thanking you.' Takarada-san straightened up and performed a neat bow. 'Now then, I do believe the main message of the card was to go up to the first floor, correct?'

'Yes, that is what it said.'

Takarada-san came out from behind the counter and said, 'Then, without further ado, I'll show you up. Right this way,' as he gestured towards the rear of the shop.

When we followed as encouraged, Takarada-san said, 'Oh, by the way . . .' as if he'd remembered something and turned to face a shelf on the right. 'The flash card decks are here. Of course, these days there are lots of convenient apps, so word on the street is that fewer people are using them.'

'That withstanding, you seem to have quite a selection.'

Including the variations of size and colour, there looked to be over a hundred types.

'Yes, I seem to be a contrarian . . . When I hear that fewer people are using an item, I want to stock even more varieties. And I think in terms of freedom to customise, analogue wins. Fortunately, among Shihodo customers, the humble paper flash card deck on a ring remains a popular item.'

'Huh . . .' A weak reaction even for me.

'This is another product from the same company, Raymay Fujii, called "Word Cards".'

At that, my wife emitted a little laugh, perhaps without really meaning to. 'Forgive me if I'm being rude, but these names – Card Memo, Word Cards – are all a bit on the nose.'

'Yes, you're quite right. They produce a significant number of things that make you think, "I can't believe you're actually able to sell under that name!" But I'm always impressed by the ingenuity evident in each of their products. These Word Cards have red and green translucent cards on the ring which you can use to hide answers highlighted with coloured markers.'

They sold memorisation aids like that when I was a student, but putting them in a flash card deck, while not a major innovation, was indeed a good idea.

'This is really amazing! Whoever thought of this is so smart. How awesome!'

Takarada-san's eyes popped wide at my wife's reaction, and he beamed. 'Not to be presumptuous, but I can tell you're

Kotomi-san's mother. She reacted exactly the same way when she saw this item – "So smart." This is just my humble opinion, but I think spotting a person's good points and then acknowledging them in a genuine way is surprisingly difficult.'

'Thank you. We at least intended to raise her to have an honest personality. Though I think, as a result, she can be a bit awkward, which causes her trouble . . .'

At 'awkward', my wife glanced at me. I can't say I didn't understand what she was trying to say. But it's not as if I wanted Kotomi to take after me in that way.

'Excuse me, going off on tangents is one of my bad habits. Now then, let me show you to the first floor. Right this way.' With that, Takarada-san led us farther towards the back.

There was a staircase against the far wall. Standing next to the sign that read: TODAY'S WORKSHOPS HAVE ENDED, Takarada-san said, 'It may be a little steep, so please do be careful,' and gestured for us to go up ahead of him.

With Takarada-san as our guide, we arrived on the first floor. The amount of floor space shouldn't have been any different from downstairs, but perhaps due to the absence of product displays and so on, it looked more spacious.

Right at the top of the stairs was a table a size larger than you'd see in an office meeting room. Beyond it were more of the same, forming a row to the back of the room.

On the edge of the closest table was a little envelope. When I picked it up, I found that it wasn't sealed, just folded closed.

As I was examining it with my wife, Takarada-san said, 'Well, that's all I have for you. This space is reserved for you until closing time. Please make yourself at home.'

I couldn't help but say, 'Err, I'm not sure I understand.'

A little smile played across his lips. 'Please see inside the envelope for details,' he said, and then, 'The bathroom is here. Also, if you need a break, please remove your shoes and sit on the *tatami*. There's tea on the table. There's also coffee from a local cafe in the thermos in the back. Feel free to enjoy whichever you prefer. I'll be on the ground floor, so do let me know if you need anything.'

'You've really gone out of your way for us . . . Thank you.' When my wife tactfully expressed her gratitude, I bowed as well.

'Not at all. Now then, take your time.' Takarada-san bowed before quietly descending to the ground floor.

It had all started the previous November. The two of us were having breakfast at our usual time when my wife received a LINE message from Kotomi: *Just so you know, I'm coming home this weekend.*

Given our work schedules, both my wife and I leave the house just after six, so we always eat breakfast around five. It was the first time we'd ever heard from her at that time of day.

It's been ten years since our daughter Kotomi moved to Tokyo on the occasion of continuing her education at university. When she first started her studies, she'd find every chance to come home, but once she started working, she must have been busy, because she only ever came for a few days over New Year's, and in recent years even that had stopped.

And when she first moved away, she was calling us practically every day.

'*Is it OK to put a jumper in the washing machine?*'

'*I'm making nikujaga – will it turn out well even if I don't have any mirin? Could I just use sugar instead?*'

Flash Card Deck

Advice on things that weren't really that important. She could have answered most of the questions with an internet search, as is common these days, but she asked us. My wife grumbled, 'Ahh, how annoying. This is what I get for never making her do a chore in her life,' even as she seemed happy to hear from her.

But, over time, the frequency of those calls went down to once a week, then every other week, then once a month, and most recently, she hadn't been calling much at all.

Instead, she'd been sending photos and little messages to my wife on LINE, but usually late at night; we could tell her waking hours were totally different from ours. Recently, though, we hadn't even been getting the LINEs.

My wife adores our only child and was on such good terms with her that they were like sisters, so she must have been feeling lonely, but she would smile and say things like, 'Well, if she's not coming home that just means she's enjoying a fulfilling life in Tokyo,' and 'The reason she doesn't call or LINE must be that she found people she can ask for advice in Tokyo.'

Now Kotomi was saying that she was coming home, and for no particular reason we could think of.

'Hmm, do you think she's sick?' I asked.

'Surely not. If she weren't feeling well, she'd see someone at a clinic in Tokyo, wouldn't she?'

I found my wife's brusque reply somewhat irritating. 'Then what do you think it is? She's never come home in November before . . . Maybe work is stressful, or she wants to switch jobs, and she wants advice?'

'Would she ask us for career advice? Even if she asked us about office politics or something difficult like needing to use

English with foreign clients, the most we could offer is, "Hang in there!" and I'm sure she knows that.'

I guess this is what it means to have no comeback, I thought.

'Then what do you think the reason is?'

She glanced at me and then heaved a sigh with an exasperated look on her face. 'Hmm, I wonder. Well, there's no point in two people with no idea thinking so hard about it. At any rate, it's the first time in a while that we'll have dinner as the three of us, so make sure you come home early. Anyhow, sorry, but I'm going to head out ahead of you.'

Left on my own, I tried to figure out what my wife's exasperated look was for, but I never did manage to understand.

'Dinner's ready!' my wife called.

I heard the padding of Kotomi's slippers as she came out of her room, along with her reply, 'OK!' As I took my seat, I reflected on how long it had been since I'd heard that sound.

There was a bottle of beer on the table. Usually we drink canned, but for a special occasion, my wife buys a big bottle. A fancier household might open a bottle of wine or champagne, but at ours it's always been beer. I simply thought my wife must have been happy Kotomi was visiting.

Kotomi took the seat across from me on the right. Up until this visit, she would always change into her high school tracksuit and make herself at home, but for some reason this time she was still in the dress and cardigan she'd arrived from Tokyo wearing.

'You wouldn't want to spill anything on that, right? It's OK to go change,' I said, setting the bottle opener against the cap, when Kotomi interjected.

'Hold on. Will you come sit down too, Mum?'

My wife silently took her place, and Kotomi straightened up.

'Before we eat, there's something I want to tell you.'

I looked at my wife. Her eyes remained fixed on her own hands.

'What is it? So formal.'

Kotomi nodded and paused for a moment before replying.

'Well, I've decided to get married.'

'What?'

Then she began telling us about the man she was marrying, and how they would be moving overseas together. It was all so sudden, I could hardly follow what she was saying.

'So we'll just get registered and not bother with stuff like engagement formalities or a reception. And then we'll be leaving the country next July. It's a little far, and I won't be able to visit very easily, so tomorrow I'm going to visit Grandpa's and Grandma's graves and say goodbye.'

The bottle of beer in front of me was dripping with condensation and must have got all warm. It didn't seem drinkable, but then, I didn't really feel like drinking anymore.

'Dear, you should say something,' my wife urged.

'Mm . . . Congratulations.'

I managed to force a response out, though well wishes weren't exactly at the top of my mind.

'Thanks . . . I was sure you'd be against it, so that was actually a bit anticlimactic.' She must have been nervous the whole time, but she finally smiled. 'OK, I'll go get changed.'

She stood up and padded back down the hallway to her room.

'Hey, are you OK?' My wife stared at me.

'Yeah . . . Yes, I'm fine.'

'That was big of you. To congratulate her.'

'... Being complimented about it doesn't really help.' I stood. 'Sorry, but do you think you could tell her I got called in to work?'

'All right. But let's go to the cemetery tomorrow together, all three of us. Please don't stay out too late.'

I threw on my coat as I listened to her voice behind me and left the house. I didn't have a destination in mind, but I figured I would just go for a walk to cool down.

Next thing I knew, I'd found a little park. Two swings, a slide, a sandpit. A few benches and a water fountain. Really, a little park.

I sat on a bench and looked at the swings. It was pitch-dark outside, and a few lamps hazily illuminated the park.

'Make sure you hold on tight!'

'I know! Oh, but slow is fine! I don't want a big shove out of nowhere!'

Kotomi was the sort of girl who was that anxious about riding a swing. And now that quiet girl would get married and go and live overseas.

When I looked up, the sky was overcast, so I couldn't even see the moon, much less the stars.

The next day, on the way back from the cemetery, I was at the wheel as usual. The plan was to not even return home but just drop Kotomi at the station directly. In the back seat, my wife was explaining the contents of a paper bag she was having Kotomi take with her.

We had just about reached the station when we hit a red light. I glanced in the rear-view mirror and said, 'Hey, Kotomi. I just have one favour to ask. I won't tell you to have a lavish reception. But I'd like you to show your mum and dad what you look like as a bride. And we need to say a proper hello to the man's parents . . . So it can be as simple as a dinner party for the two families, but please have some kind of wedding.'

My eyes met those of my wife via the rear-view mirror. Hers were angry, seeming to say, *What's that for all of a sudden?!*

For a little while, there was no reply. When a honk from the car behind us brought me back to myself, I saw the light was green. I hurriedly pushed the pedal, and Kotomi answered at the same time.

'OK . . . I'll ask him. I don't know what he'll say, but I'll do what you want if I can. Just please give me a little time. Once the arrangements are made, I'll get in touch.'

With that, Kotomi went back to Tokyo.

Then it must have been six months or so? Citing work, she didn't come home for New Year's, and my wife and I did our best not to mention her. To be honest, I had pretty much given up. Then an envelope arrived. It was addressed to the two of us, and the sender was Kotomi.

Inside was a flash card deck and limited express train tickets.

'What's this?'

The flash card deck was bound by a band attached with grommets. I opened it to find rows of characters written neatly in brilliant blue ink.

Though neat, the handwriting had its quirks – it was Kotomi's.

Dear Dad, Mum,
I'm sorry for the long wait. I'm writing to you because everything is set for the wedding.

After that were the date, time and venue. The location was a historic restaurant at a hotel near Ginza in Tokyo.

'Noon on a Saturday . . . We should go the night before just to be safe.'

I quickly grabbed my planner out of my bag and confirmed my schedule. I was surprised to see that I had already requested paid time off the Thursday and Friday of the week in question.

'This is the week we . . .'

'Yes, the week I had you take PTO so we could go on a trip to celebrate our coral anniversary.'

Apparently Kotomi and my wife had worked together to choose the date.

'So that's why . . . I *thought* something was strange. We didn't do anything for silver, but then you suggested we go somewhere to celebrate thirty-five years . . .'

'Hee-hee, well, yeah.'

The second card read:

Since you're coming from so far away, I'd like you to see some of the sights in Tokyo. First come to the hotel where the wedding will be held. I'll tell you what happens next from there.

There was also a leaflet showing how to get to the hotel from the nearest station.

'Hmm, this is a bit . . .'

'It's fine, isn't it? We haven't gone overnight anywhere just the two of us since our honeymoon.'

I couldn't help but stare at my wife's happy face.

Flash Card Deck

The previous day, we had left for Tokyo as planned. We followed the map to the hotel, and when we were shown to our room, we found a little envelope. Inside was another card like we'd been sent in the post.

Dear Dad, Mum,
You must be tired after your long trip. After you rest a bit, please go back down to the lobby. At the far end of reception is the concierge desk. Find Haibara-san and say hello.

'I wonder what this is about,' I said to my wife as I showed her the card.

'Who knows? For now, let's just do as she says and go to the concierge desk.'

I nodded in silence and added the card to the deck from Kotomi.

'I guess these are for taking notes? If you put them all on a ring like this, you don't have to worry about losing any.'

My wife sighed with a dry laugh. 'Right. You get bothered when things aren't in their proper places, so she must have taken your personality into account when coming up with this.'

'You didn't give her any hints?'

'Heavens, no. I didn't do a thing.'

I looked down at the card in my hand again. It had definitely been written by Kotomi, but the high-quality paper and blue ink had a mature air about them, and I felt like I'd been shown a side of my daughter I'd never seen before.

In the end, I couldn't relax, so after unpacking, we went straight down to the lobby.

When we asked for Haibara-san at the concierge desk,

it seemed Kotomi had previously met with her, and she took good care of us. Appointments for clothes and hair, a taxi to the Kabukiza Theatre, where we attended the evening performance in box seats. Dinner was a luxurious shokado bento served at intermission.

Everywhere we went there was an envelope waiting for us with a flash card from Kotomi inside. When we returned to the hotel, Haibara-san met us with an envelope and said, 'This is the last one for today.' The card inside read: *There's a lounge on the top floor. I ordered you the cocktail I recommend.*

When we got out of the lift and entered the lounge, we found that a window table had been reserved for us. The view below was half Imperial Palace forest and moat, half the twinkling neon lights of Ginza.

'This is all such a dream. Do you think these excesses will come back to bite us later?' said my wife with the cocktail sitting before her.

'I was just about to say the same thing . . .'

She smiled as if to say, *That's why I said it!* 'But I wonder if it's really OK. Haibara-san said Kotomi is paying.'

That had been on my mind, too.

'Well, I suppose all we can do is put more cash in the congratulations envelope on the day of the wedding. If we insist on paying, it will only make things awkward for Haibara-san.'

'True. That said, I am enjoying myself. We should come to Tokyo together once in a while. I'd like to see more kabuki. And Takarazuka and the Shiki Theatre Company too.'

'I didn't know you were interested in theatre.'

My wife nodded with a soft, gentle smile. 'But wow, it's already been ten years since Kotomi left home . . . I think part of me thought she would come back at some point and the three of us would live together again. But now she's getting married, and they'll be creating a home of their own . . . There's no point in waiting anymore. We should act like we're newlyweds again and have some fun.'

Her thinking that way surprised me.

'You really want to do that with me?'

'. . . Huh?! What are you talking about?'

'I mean, you're on a committee backed by the mayor, and people want you to run in the next city council election . . . I'm just a humble company employee who had to retire from his management position . . . You're the kind of person an editor comes all the way out from Tokyo to see. There's no reason you would have to stick with me . . .'

I couldn't really find any other words.

'You dummy . . .'

'I am a dummy, though – that's the thing.' Even I was put off by how childish I was acting.

'If you don't want me to do the publishing deal, I won't do it. I could quit the committee, too. I'm sure there are plenty of people who could replace me. But you only have one wife, and that's me, right?'

'. . . What?'

'We've been together thirty-five years – through thick and thin. Are you saying I should start over from scratch with someone else? That's not funny!'

I felt like my tears might overflow in spite of myself.

Maybe the low lighting in the lounge gave me courage – I took my wife's hands in mine.

'Oh, so bold!'

Notes from the Ginza Shihodo Stationery Shop

'... Yeah, maybe I'm a little drunk,' I mumbled to hide my embarrassment.

My wife smiled in a way that was almost a wince. 'Stop confusing me by saying things that make no sense.'

It was all I could do to silently nod.

And then, I wonder how long we were holding hands. The candle burning on the table got a lot shorter.

Finally, I was able to look squarely at my wife and say, 'So...'

'Hm?'

'I was scared.'

'Scared? Of what?'

'That everyone might leave me behind... Kotomi's getting married and moving overseas; you're becoming such a success, I feel like I might not even know you anymore soon... I got scared I might end up left all alone in that house.'

'... You really are a dummy.'

I nodded. 'But I feel a bit better. I'm sorry I said that weird stuff. I want you to not worry about it and keep working the same way you have been. And do the book, too, of course.'

'OK...'

I let go of her hand and straightened up. 'Maybe it's annoying to say, but I'm happy to be continuing life with you. And: do your best!'

'OK, thanks. I'm happy too.'

And then today. We left the hotel, strolled around the Imperial Palace and after lunch at the yoshoku restaurant, we arrived at Shihodo.

'Hey, hurry up and show me what's inside.'

'Right, just a second.'

Flash Card Deck

I opened the envelope. As expected, it was another card.

Sorry to make you walk all over the place, but this is the last stop for today. All that's left is to go back to the hotel, eat dinner and go to bed. So please stick with me a little longer.

I lined up some photo memories in order, heading towards the back of the room. Please take your time looking at them.

My wife and I exchanged a look. When I let my eyes slide from there down the table, I saw more flash cards and white papers.

'Those papers are the photos, I guess?'

'Probably. And there are quite a few of them, huh?'

There were six worktables in a line leading to the back of the room, and they all had multiple papers on them.

'What, you didn't know about this?'

'No!'

I walked over to the first photo and flipped it over to find Kotomi as a newborn.

'She's so small!' we inadvertently said in unison and then laughed.

Next to the photo were two more flash cards, also facing down. The first card said her birthday and then: *Kotomi is born! 3,023 grams.* There was a little sticky note on it that read: *The photos are all sized to fit the flash card deck. Please put them on the ring with the cards as you go.* When I picked up the photo, I saw it had been hole-punched on the left edge.

'What's all this for?'

'Who knows . . .? But business card-sized photos don't exist, so she must have taken pictures of the photos in the album with her phone or something and then printed them.'

'Ah.'

The second card had more words on it.

I heard it was a hard birth for Mum. Dad had to work and didn't think he would be there, but I guess I held out? He was able to make it in time.

'Right, right, oh yeah. You kept calling me on that mobile phone we'd just bought . . . even though I said it hurt too bad to talk.'

'Ack . . .'

'But just like she wrote here, I remember quite well how she was born as if she had been waiting for you to get to the hospital.'

I took the cards and photos from my wife and put them on the ring with the rest of the deck.

Next to that was a shot taken in front of a *torii*.

'This is her first shrine visit.'

I was in a suit and my wife was holding Kotomi.

'Fast asleep. Right, right, either because she was out of sorts or because the drums and bells scared her, she cried all through the prayer and then didn't make so much as a peep after the moment it ended. The priest was miffed, but the shrine maiden was kind enough to say, "Please don't worry about it – a baby's job is to cry, after all. It's proof she's healthy."'

'Oh yeah . . .'

After that was her first Hina Matsuri.

'We haven't put out the dolls in years.'

'Well, when the girl we're celebrating isn't around, there doesn't feel like much of a point.'

Flash Card Deck

'True . . . Come to think of it, I haven't got to eat your *chirashizushi* in ages, either.'

Some wryness slipped into my wife's smile. 'It's a lot of work to make, you know. But we make it every year for the daycare, so I suppose I get my fix there. Have you missed it? Is that what you're saying?'

'Yeah, I guess; if possible, I'd like to have it. They sell it at the shop, of course, but it's nothing like home-made.'

Kotomi, who had just gained the ability to support her own head, was so precious sitting in front of the Hina Matsuri doll display. She was smiling, holding a bag of festive crackers, with no idea yet at all what the girls' festival was about.

The pictures continued: a shot of her with an elephant at the zoo, the three of us having a picnic and so on. Then one of her chomping into a cake that said *Happy 1st Birthday!*, her face full of cream.

'Oh, I remember when she did that!' said my wife, picking up the photo. 'We had them do soy cream so it would be OK for babies, but cream is still cream. She got her sticky fingers into everything, and it was so hard to clean up afterwards . . .'

There was a single flash card to go with all these pictures.

One full year! It's clear from a glance at the photo album that you showered me with love.

'Of course we did, why would she write that?' I said, feeling awkwardly happy as I handed my wife the card.

'I don't think it's a matter of "of course" at all.'

'No? Isn't it only natural for parents to love their children?'

My wife set the card back on the table, shaking her head

slowly. 'It's not. I've come into contact with lots of parents and children at the daycare. I've seen mothers fret that they can't bring themselves to love their child even though they gave birth to them, and plenty of fathers can't seem to take an interest in their kids even though they're related by blood. The fact that we're both able to love Kotomi from the bottom of our hearts and she's able to love us back is actually such a blessing.'

'... Is that right?'

'Plus, some couples do nothing but fight.'

'Even though they got married because they liked each other?'

My wife nodded without saying anything. *That pursed-lip expression is one she's made since the first time we met*, I thought.

After graduating high school, I got a job at a local transportation company. At first, I was a provisional hire, so to make money I did whatever they needed: loading cargo, washing and maintaining the trucks, organising paperwork. In my free time, I went to driving school, and once I got my standard licence, I expressed my wish to drive a small truck, so in my second year I was hired full-time as a driver.

I met Miho back then, when she was working at the company canteen.

Not yet a dietician and without even a cooking licence, she was assigned mainly prep work, like cleaning and chopping ingredients and washing the pots and dishes. There was something green about her, but the way she threw herself into her work really impressed me.

One day, I spotted Miho sweating as she carried heavy boxes of freshly delivered ingredients into the kitchen. I casually picked up a box of potatoes.

Flash Card Deck

'You can't do that!'

I turned around at the stern voice to find Miho standing there glaring at me with her lips tightly pursed.

'Err, I just . . . It seemed like you were having a hard time.'

'I don't mean to offend you, but you're a driver, right? If you tired yourself out helping me, that would be a big problem. It could cause an accident.'

'That's a bit dramatic . . . I don't know about one of the older hands, but I'm still young – I'll be all right. Plus, I may not look like it, but I'm a pro cargo handler . . . so . . . You don't have to take it so seriously.'

Miho was so petite that she had to look up at me. 'I'm sorry I shouted . . . But this is my job. I can't let you do it for me.'

'Hmm, then how about this? When I help you with something, you can give me extra rice. Even if I'm tired, I'll be fine if I eat a lot. That's fair, then, right?'

My one-sided appeal must have amused her. Miho's eyes popped wide, and she abruptly burst out laughing. Listening to her carefree laughter, I started to find the whole thing amusing myself and ended up laughing with her.

'You're pretty funny.'

'What! Am I . . .? I always thought I was on the serious side.'

'That goofy seriousness is what's so funny . . .' she answered, and then came more of her sunny laughter, like ringing bells.

We grew closer like that, bit by bit, and after dating for a few years, we got married. By that time, Miho had acquired both her cooking licence and registered dietician certification, as well as the position she'd always wanted at a public daycare. I steadily saved up money, went back to driving school for my large motor vehicle licence and started doing long-haul trucking.

Those days were smooth sailing, but for some reason we couldn't seem to have children.

'They say a baby is a blessing from heaven, right?' I tried to keep things upbeat, but Miho was really stressing about it.

'I work at a daycare because I love kids, yet I can't get pregnant. I'm glad I get to work surrounded by little kids, but . . . lately the number of mothers even younger than me has grown, and it stings to see them all happily walking home holding hands with their children.' When she spoke about this, she would always start to cry.

'Ah . . . Then what about switching jobs? You could even come back to the canteen. And I realise I've said it before, but just because you want kids doesn't mean you'll be able to have them. It's a matter of luck.'

'But you like kids too, don't you? Weren't you saying you wanted enough to start a basketball team? Even football or baseball, you said. So . . .'

To save money for the future, we'd stayed living in a single-room, six-tatami-mat apartment in an old wooden building even after getting married. How many times did we have that same conversation in that little room?

Miho would collapse into sobs, and I'd hold her, stroking her hair until we fell asleep, completely exhausted. Our life continued like that for quite a long time.

The change came abruptly. Our landlord said he wanted to demolish the old building to construct something new and asked if we would move. 'We'll give you a good deal at one of my other properties,' he said, and so we moved into a three-bedroom place with a living room, dining room and kitchen. Changing from a place that was hot in the summer and draughty in the winter, where the hallway creaked with every step, to a place with south-facing windows brightened up Miho's depressed mood.

We splurged on all new furniture, curtains and bedding and I bought all the kitchen gadgets that Miho said she wanted to use in the gorgeous kitchen with the built-in three-burner stove. We always struggled to get paid holiday at the same time, but we managed to pull it off and had fun shopping with the money we'd saved up.

Maybe that cheerful lifestyle did us good. One day, Miho stopped me just as I'd got out of the bath. 'Do you have a minute?'

'What is it?'

I sat down and she took something out of an envelope. It said 'Maternal and Child Health Handbook'.

'What's that?'

'Oh, c'mon! Don't you get it?'

I stared at Miho's face. 'You mean . . . you're pregnant?'

'. . . Yeah.'

'Wh-wh-wh . . . whaaaat . . .!' I jumped up and started pacing around. 'R-really? We're gonna have a baby?'

'Yeah.'

'Woo-hoo!'

It might have been the first time in my life that I literally jumped for joy. I didn't do anything like that when I got my driver's licence or when I passed the test for large motor vehicles. When I looked at Miho, she was crying.

'I thought we'd never be able to have children. I'd given up . . . But lately I've been feeling so queasy . . . And when I went to the doctor just to make sure nothing was wrong, they said, "Congratulations!" I couldn't even believe it at first . . .'

'... Uh-huh, uh-huh.'

I wanted to say something more considerate, but I didn't have the words.

*

The next photograph was of the three of us next to a sign celebrating Kotomi's graduation from daycare. Next to it was a flash card, of course. It read *Memories of Daycare*, and there was another beneath it.

I attended the daycare where Mum worked from ages one to five. I was so happy to get to be with Mum all the time.

There was a picture of my wife pushing a buggy heading to daycare and a picture of her pedalling a bicycle with Kotomi in a helmet riding in the child seat.

'Nowadays, it's not so rare to have your first child at that age, but back then, it was young mothers as far as the eye could see. I felt somehow ashamed . . . And all the daycare workers called me *Sensei*. I mean, I know it's because I'm a registered dietician, but . . .'

'It gave me great peace of mind, knowing you two were together,' I replied.

The next photo was one of Kotomi grinning ear to ear as she chowed down on some food.

Everyone loved the tasty lunches Mum made! I found out there have been over 500 kids who grew up eating her lunches. I was so happy to get to eat Mum's cooking for breakfast and dinner too, but it sure was hard to get used to other people's cooking after leaving home . . .

Flash Card Deck

Next to Kotomi's picture were others: a bunch of kids eating lunch, my wife having a meeting with the other cooks, taste-testing, etc.

'I'm surprised she had all these pictures of you at work!'

'She must have found them in her daycare graduation album.'

And there were other photographs next to the flash card. They started with baby Kotomi napping in the nursery room, then her a little older zooming around the daycare garden, and included a shot of her passionate performance as the wolf in *The Three Little Pigs*.

'This is the old daycare building in these photographs, right? It's kinda nostalgic.'

'Yeah, they rebuilt it five years ago, huh ... Of course it needed earthquake-proofing, but it's also just safer for small children as a whole now. To be honest, though, I was a little sad – it was the place where Kotomi and I went together for so many years.'

I wanted to say something but I couldn't find the words.

'Oh, this looks interesting.'

I'd been gazing absent-mindedly at the flash card in my hand when my wife spoke from a little farther down. The flash card she was holding read *Dates with Dad!* The one next to it read:

Mum sometimes went to work even on the weekends. On those days, Dad took me out. To the amusement park, hiking, to watch a film, shopping at a department store – the person I've been on the most dates with is definitely Dad.

Around it were pictures of Kotomi waving from atop a horse on a merry-go-round and her biting into an awkwardly shaped *onigiri* I'd made.

Notes from the Ginza Shihodo Stationery Shop

'Looks like fun . . . Those days, I was so busy it was hard to line up our days off. I'm so grateful that you took her out all over. Whenever she would tell me about where you went or how much fun you had, I was happy but a bit envious at the same time.'

'Sorry . . .'

She smiled and shook her head. 'Why are you apologising? Once she was in middle and high school, you went back to being a student and all the two of you ever did was study. I felt the most left out during that period!'

I got hired at a small local transportation company, but no sooner had we merged with another company in the industry that we started being absorbed by ever bigger companies, and before I knew it, I was an employee at what was known as a major corporation.

The division of driving work became more regimented, so instead of coming and going on the fly like I used to, the demand was to drive the designated route at the designated time. I had enjoyed driving roads I'd never been on and seeing new scenery, so the new system really took the joy out of the job for me.

And driving meant staying seated for long periods of time, so once I was over forty I began to suffer lower back pain. At first, I tried to ignore it, but it only grew worse.

One day, I made up my mind to talk to my boss, and he was empathetic. Fortunately, thanks to my twenty-plus years of no accidents or traffic violations, I was able to be moved from the truck to a job in safety management.

'The only thing is that you'll lose all the benefits that came with being a driver, so your pay will go down.'

Flash Card Deck

Kotomi had just started middle school, so there would be a lot of expenses coming up, like cram school and other costs associated with heading to high school.

'I don't think you'll have any problem performing the safety management duties, Chida. I know you have the potential to head up a big distribution centre in the future. The only thing is that if you're looking for desk job promotions . . . you need a university degree.'

Looking down at my HR profile, he paused for a moment.

'What do you think? You graduated high school. Would you be interested in trying to get a degree at night or through a correspondence school? Oh, and we can get the company to help pay tuition. There's actually an age limit, but if I make a recommendation, it won't matter.'

That night, I told my wife what my boss had said.

'Sounds like a great opportunity, no?'

'Do you really think so? I could try to cover the difference with overtime, but it's a twenty per cent pay cut. And if I actually go to night school, I won't be able to do overtime.'

She looked down at her freshly steeped tea and shook her head.

'If the alternative is ruining your body, then what choice do you really have? Listen, you may think you've done a good job of hiding it, but I know you've been taking painkillers. If you keep driving with your body in that condition and cause an accident, then what? You won't be able to undo it. And as for the money, we'll manage. We just have to live within our means, that's all.'

'But we have lots of expenses coming up for Kotomi, right?'

'Are you really using Kotomi as an excuse? Plus, if you really care about Kotomi, you should get out of the truck and study with an eye to the future.'

It doesn't happen often, but sometimes my wife argues in a way that is impossible for me to counter.

'. . . But studying for entrance exams at my age? Do you think I can pass? Do you even remember anything you studied in high school? The thought of starting over from scratch is honestly pretty depressing.'

'There, see? That's how you really feel. So just say you don't like studying so you don't want to go to university. Don't make excuses about how we need to spend money on Kotomi.'

Once she said that, I couldn't give up. I started studying that very day, but the mock test I tried to take felt like utter gobbledygook. With no other choice, I started over with middle school English and maths.

Meanwhile, during the day I had to get used to desk work, a parade of new tasks that was its own challenge. How could I study most effectively around my commute, bathroom breaks and bathtime? The answer I arrived at was flash cards.

'You two look so much alike here,' my wife murmured softly. She was pointing at a picture of Kotomi and me sitting at the *kotatsu* studying. The flash card next to it said, *Studying!*

All I remember about middle school is my club stuff and studying with Dad. I'm pretty sure we studied every day from 9 to 11? I tutored him in maths and English; he tutored me in Japanese, science and social studies. By teaching each other, we both got smarter?!

Flash Card Deck

My way of studying was ever so Showa period – brute-force memorisation. Kotomi, on the other hand, reasoned things out to remember them, and our respective strong subjects reflected the difference in our methods.

'If you have time to make flash cards, wouldn't it be better to do more drills?'

I ignored Kotomi's advice and continued relying on flash cards. And it seemed like that method suited me, because my scores did slowly improve.

'I mean, maybe, but if I go through an exercise book, then I need to buy another exercise book, right? Flash cards, on the other hand, you can use over and over, so I think they're a cost-conscious choice. And I can also study on buses and trains.'

'. . . Well, I won't knock your style, but I think flash cards are most effective when you're making them rather than using them.'

I looked down at the cards off their ring, scattered across the kotatsu.

'I'll give you that. When I made "INTERESTING", for example, I was writing too big, so the "ING" is so tiny. Lamenting that in my head, I flipped it over and wrote the "*kyo*" from "*kyomibukai*" too big, which meant I had to write the "*i*" super small. The whole thing made me feel really stupid, but thanks to that, I remembered the word in one shot.'

'Right?'

While we had exchanges like this, my wife would always bring us cocoa or warm milk.

'All right, you two, take a look at the clock. You have school and work tomorrow, right?'

We competed to see who could get the best scores, and

eventually I got into the university I was aiming for. It was two years after I started studying. When I showed my wife and Kotomi the notification that came in the post, they were thrilled for me.

'It's kind of amazing that you could pass a university entrance exam while working full-time.'

'Thanks. But this means I'll have to keep studying while I work for a while . . .'

I looked down at the notification letter. Along with the faculty and department, it said 'evening division'.

'. . . Right, so you'll keep studying at night.' It sounded like Kotomi's voice suddenly got quieter.

'Yeah, regular classes are weekday nights, but apparently we do physical education and whatnot on Sunday when the daytime students aren't using the fields or gym. Can I really handle PE at my age?' I said it lightly, but Kotomi gazed at me intently.

'Do your best, Dad. I'll do my best, too. First for high school entrance exams, and then university.'

'Hm, I think you'll be OK, Kotomi. After all, you've been teaching your dad maths and English.'

'Don't exaggerate! That was only the first few months. Oh, that reminds me. I have a favour to ask . . .'

Kotomi's expression looked more serious than I'd ever seen it, and I straightened up my posture.

'What is it?'

'Um . . . you still have the flash card decks you made, right?'

'Oh, yeah.'

Really, once you've learned the content, the cards' purpose has been fulfilled, but I had the feeling that if I threw them away,

Flash Card Deck

I'd forget everything I'd worked so hard to remember, so I kept them in a cardboard box.

'Could I have them?'

I can't say I expected that.

'You want those old things?'

'Yeah, your writing has its quirks, but you wrote a lot on them, right? I'm sure I'll learn a whole lot just looking through them, and when I feel like slacking off, I think remembering how hard you worked might help me push through.'

I was sort of happy to hear her accept my single-mindedness in a roundabout way.

'I'd be happy for you to have them.'

Starting the next day, I took about a week and organised all the card decks I'd made over the previous two years. The classical Japanese and English vocabulary cards I struggled with so much were dirty, and some of the cards' holes had ripped. I repaired the holes, rewrote letters that had blurred and arranged them by subject and the order I studied them in. And I remember back then, too, being impressed with how handy and neat it was to be able to put the rings on a string to keep all the English with English, history with history and so on.

'It was only ten years ago, but it feels like much longer.'

I returned to myself at the sound of my wife's voice. Suddenly, I saw a photo of Kotomi standing next to the sign celebrating her graduation from high school. After that were a bunch of pictures I'd never seen before. The flash card said, *The Tokyo Me You Two Don't Know*.

'Ahh, it's true.'

Next was a picture of Kotomi smiling awkwardly in a suit she'd just had made, taken against the backdrop of the red-brick university building. Graduation had only been a month prior, but she already looked more grown-up, partially due to trading in her ponytail for a bold new shorter cut.

Kotomi – perhaps at her part-time job? – wearing the charming, mandated outfit and carrying cake and a teapot on a tray. Kotomi in her team uniform holding her lacrosse stick with a smile. Kotomi – perhaps interning somewhere? – giving some sort of presentation in a suit. Kotomi – perhaps on holiday with friends? – at sights around Japan, and even photos that seemed to have been taken overseas. It was true, they were all versions of her I'd never seen before.

The flash card next to them said, *I'd always wanted to live alone, but some nights I felt so lonely I cried.*

'If she was that lonely, she could have just come home . . .'

My wife shook her head as she took the card from me. 'No, Kotomi hangs in there, just like you.'

Kotomi's high school graduation and my university graduation happened in the same year, coinciding in March. We had to attend two ceremonies with just a three-day gap: mine was the 7th and hers was the 10th. To celebrate for the both of us, my wife prepared *sekihan* and a whole red snapper on the day of Kotomi's graduation.

'OK, let's have a toast.'

My wife took the cap off the bottle of beer and poured some into my cup. As I poured a cup for my wife, Kotomi poured herself some ginger ale.

Once everyone was ready, our eyes all met.

'Dear, you have to say a few words or something. A toast, c'mon!'

Flash Card Deck

It may have just been a modest gathering of our three family members, but I'd never been good at formal addresses.

'Uhh, Kotomi, congratulations on your graduation. And getting into university. You worked hard. So . . . cheers!'

My wife and Kotomi repeated, 'Cheers,' and took a sip from their cups. I don't have a particularly high tolerance for alcohol, but I drained my glass in one go. It was without a doubt the best glass of beer in my life.

'Congrats to you too, Dad. I can't believe you managed to keep going four years while working full-time . . . I can't very well slack off when you're sending me to a day school,' Kotomi said as she poured me another glass of beer.

'My feelings about graduating are complicated . . . happy, but also kind of sad. It was a bit rough at first, but the classes were interesting. I guess I probably felt that way because I thought I would be able to put my knowledge into practice on the job. And I had tons of younger classmates and made new friends.'

'Come to think of it, you do seem more youthful lately.' My wife smiled as she handed me a bowl of sekihan.

'I ended up doing it later in life, but I'm really glad you gave me the push to get my degree. And, Kotomi, you'll have your own life starting tomorrow. I want you to enjoy every minute of your university days in Tokyo.'

'I will. Thanks Dad, and Mum.'

My wife had been holding it together so far, but at this point she was dabbing at the corners of her eyes with the hem of her apron.

'But if it gets too rough, you can always come home,' I said. 'You wanted to go to Tokyo, so I didn't stand in your way.

Notes from the Ginza Shihodo Stationery Shop

But, to be honest, I'm worried about sending you there, and I'll miss you. I was born here, raised here and don't really know anywhere else, so Tokyo might as well be a foreign country to me . . . We'll keep your room just as it is, forever – you can come home and use it just as you always have, whenever you want. So if things get tough, you can come home.'

'. . . OK.' The word fell from Kotomi's lips as if mustering her voice had been a struggle.

'Honestly! If you put it like that, it's even harder for her to come back. This is a chance to celebrate, and you're turning it into a wake!'

'What! You're the one who started crying!'

'But I couldn't help it when I saw Kotomi's face.'

'Whaaat? It's my fault now?!'

We all exchanged a look and laughed at how we'd fallen into our usual pattern. It felt like just the other day, but it had already been ten years since then.

When I glanced at my watch, I saw we'd been looking at photos for two hours. There was only one table of photos and flash cards left.

Me as a Working Adult, said one of the cards on the table.

Once I got out into the world, I realised anew how amazing you are, Dad, Mum. Working is so hard. I'm sure you've both been through lots of hard times I know nothing about . . .

The photograph next to that must have been the day she started her job? She wore the simple black suit of new recruits and a serious expression. There were also a few pictures of her that seemed to have been taken at work.

'I can hardly imagine working in such a big city as Tokyo . . . It must have been hard for her.'

'Yeah . . . And it seemed like her job involved a lot of correspondence with people overseas. They probably don't do things the Japanese way, so there must have been a lot for her to worry about.'

We flipped over each photo, then picked it up, proceeding down the table. The flash card ring in my hand was nearly full.

At the end of the table, there seemed to be one final card. It said, *Me and Daisuke-san*, and continued in neat characters.

It was my third year of work. I got to know Daisuke-san as my boss in my new department. He's very intense about work, and at first I didn't like him, but over time I found myself attracted to the way he applied himself so earnestly in every situation. I think it's probably because he reminded me of Dad.

The photo placed alongside that card featured Kotomi and – perhaps they were having a meeting? – a man in a suit.

'This must be Daisuke-kun?'

'Mmm, probably.'

We'd heard from Kotomi that he was quite a bit older. He seemed a capable worker and had been selected as the CEO of an affiliate company abroad. Apparently he had been married once in his twenties, but they had divorced before having any children. *He seems an awful lot older . . . Will it work out? Isn't it possible that he's divorced because he's not cut out for married life?* I had nothing but concerns, but I purposely left them unvoiced.

Once I put the photo of the two of them on the flash card ring, it was full. I handed it to my wife and practically collapsed into a chair at the big table near the window.

'Somehow I'm exhausted...'

Just as the grumble left my lips, I glanced towards the end of the table and saw the coffee cups, sugar bowl and milk creamer on a stainless-steel tray. And a thermos next to it.

In the middle of the table was a single envelope – not the small size that had been used to deliver the flash cards, but a full-sized envelope fit for Western stationery. It said, *Dad, Mum*, in Kotomi's handwriting on the front.

As she took a seat in the other chair at the table, my wife picked up the envelope.

'This is from her, too.'

'I can tell from the handwriting,' I answered as I accepted it from her.

'So open it.'

When I flipped it over, it was sealed tight.

'I'm kind of scared to read it,' I said without really meaning to, and my wife nodded deeply.

'Well, for now, why don't we have some of the coffee they've prepared for us?'

I shook my head, staring vacantly at the envelope. 'No, let's read it first. If I have coffee, I'll want to read it even less.'

As a courteous touch, there was a pen tray on the table with a letter opener on it. I put the tip of the elegantly curved knife into the envelope and was able to open it smoothly, with a pleasant amount of resistance against my hand.

Flash Card Deck

Inside was a sheet of Western stationery folded in half. The off-white paper had some thickness to it and such good structural integrity that when I unfolded it, the fold was hardly noticeable. The ink was bright but had depth to it – a colour reminiscent of the night sky or the deep sea.

Dear Dad, Mum,

I had you look back over the twenty-eight years since I was born.

Did you have fun? I enjoyed selecting the photos and writing the messages.

First of all, thank you for allowing me to get married.

It's a big age split, and Daisuke-san has been divorced, so I was sure you would be against it. When you said, 'Congratulations,' I was so happy, I cried.

The reason I chose Daisuke-san is that I thought we could be a married couple like you two, two people who support each other no matter what happens.

When I had to give my first presentation in English, Daisuke-san made memorisation notes for me – using a flash card deck. When I saw that, I remembered the flash card decks Dad made, the ones he gave me. Daisuke-san's writing was neat, and he gave detailed advice like, 'Leave a beat here,' or 'Emphasise the accent here at the start' – it really helped me out. Up to that point, I hadn't really been a fan, but after that I began to notice him more.

Starting next month, I'll be farther away than Tokyo, in a whole different country. I'm nervous about whether I'll be able to make it in a land where I don't know anyone except Daisuke-san. But I'm your daughter, so I think I'll be OK. We'll do our best to create a home like you two have. I doubt I'll be able to come visit very often, but please be patient. If I ever get too lonely or have some sort of trouble, I'll write a letter. I'd be happy if you could write a reply – because I can read it over and over.

Finally, thank you so much for everything these past twenty-eight years. You took such good care of me. I'm so glad I was born as your daughter. I still lack experience, so I'm sure I'll be a burden on you in some way or other. But I'll do my best, so I hope you'll keep supporting me.

Kotomi

I handed the stationery to my wife and wordlessly stood. When I looked out the window, I saw a gentle breeze was blowing, and the leaves of the willow trees were rustling. Squinting a bit, I could make out the face of an older man with moist eyes reflected in the window glass. It took a few moments for me to realise it was my own. It looked so comedically pathetic that I burst out laughing.

'What's so funny about your own face? C'mon, have some coffee and pull yourself together,' my wife calmly admonished.

'You're always so collected. I don't know how you can read a letter like that and not be moved at all,' I grumbled, but when I turned around, my wife's cheeks were damp. 'Oh . . . I feel a bit better now. I thought I was the only one crying.'

'What! I do cry sometimes, you know.'

'Come to think of it, you used to cry a lot.'

My wife's lips curled slightly, and she shook her head as

she poured us coffee. 'I think you're quicker to cry than me these days.'

'... That's true.'

I wiped away my tears with the back of a hand and sat down at the table to take a sip of the freshly poured coffee.

'Yum.'

I'd said it before I realised. While the roasters had managed to restrain both the bitterness and acidity, the fragrance passing through my nose was rich, and even I, who usually only drink canned or instant coffee, could tell from a single sip that it was quality.

'It really is delicious. I wonder if we could enjoy the same flavour at home if we bought some beans.'

'Hmm, there might be a trick to preparing it. If we want to drink it again, we can get Takarada-san to tell us which cafe it's from and just come back to Ginza.'

We looked at each other and giggled. I felt better after crying somehow.

'So, there's something I wanted to ask you about ...' I said.

'What is it? You don't need to be so formal.'

I set my cup on the table.

'We're going to meet Daisuke-kun's parents for the first time tomorrow, right? I took some notes about what we should say in our address ... I mean, I just looked up a typical wedding speech online. But I started to feel like maybe that wouldn't be good enough, as Kotomi's parents ...'

'Oh, so that's what you were looking up. I could tell you were researching something.'

I nodded. 'Yeah, because you seemed busy ...'

'Right ... So what do you want to do?'

'I'd like to think together about how to change it. I don't seem to have any talent for writing, but you've been offered a book deal. Lend me your wisdom.'

My wife rolled her eyes. 'Of course I'll look at it with you, but I don't feel confident either.'

As we were sitting there stiffly, a voice called out from behind us.

'Excuse me.'

I turned around to see Takarada-san approaching from the stairwell.

When I rushed to my feet, he urged us to stay seated. 'Please, please, stay as you are. If you're having a coffee break, this is good timing. Some eclairs just arrived from the same cafe. Enjoy them with the coffee.'

He took white plates off the tray he was carrying and set them in front of us.

'Oh my, they look delicious,' my wife murmured spontaneously.

'They go very well with coffee. I brought you forks, but I also included moist towelettes – I recommend picking them up with your hands and chomping right in. The custard filling is rich without being overly sweet and pairs exquisitely with the bitter chocolate coating the choux pastry.' Takarada-san smiled warmly.

'You've thought of everything . . . Thank you so much.' My wife stood and bowed low. I hurriedly lowered my head as well.

'Please raise your heads. I only prepared everything according to Kotomi-san's instructions. She's a wonderful young lady who cares deeply about her parents. And I hear there's a wedding tomorrow? Congratulations!'

Flash Card Deck

When I glanced at my wife next to me, our eyes met. I gave her a slight nod.

'She is so admirable, and because of that, we want to make sure to give a speech at the ceremony that won't embarrass her, but neither my wife nor I have experience giving an address at such a formal occasion. We're completely overwhelmed...'

Takarada-san listened, his mild expression unchanging, and then gently shook his head. 'My sense is that ... no matter the content of the address, if it's the bride's parents speaking in earnest, it'll be great. Especially since you're the parents of such a wonderful daughter as Kotomi-san, if you say proudly what's in your heart, it's sure to be an address of the finest quality. I don't think you need to be particular about the format. As long as you choose each word with care and make sure the message is easily understood, that's plenty. That said, there seem to be many people with the same worry, and they sometimes come here for advice. Given that experience, I may be able to be of some small assistance. First, please take a seat.'

We sat back down as encouraged, and the scene out of the window came into view. The sun had started to set, and the Ginza alley was dyed amber.

* * *

On an alleyway in Ginza was the stationery shop Shihodo. When the manager, Ken Takarada, looked out towards the street, he saw the poster girl of the cafe Hohozue, Ryoko, receiving a bundle of post from the delivery person.

'Ken-chan, sorry to keep you waiting for your lunch. The post came, too, so I picked it up for you.'

Handing the rubber-banded bundle of post to Ken, Ryoko set

up a little table next to the till, put a cloth over it and began laying out the sandwich she'd brought. As Ken was going through the envelopes, he noticed one letter in particular.

'Oh, this one's from quite far away,' he murmured and used a letter opener to cut the seal.

'Who's it from?'

'Kotomi-san, who got married in June.'

'Oh, that pretty lady. If I remember correctly, she moved overseas with her husband immediately after the wedding...?'

'Yes, that seems to be where she's writing from.'

There was a photograph in the envelope along with the letter. It featured her in her wedding dress, flanked by her parents, Tetsuo and Miho. The three of them were smiling peacefully, and Ken and Ryoko couldn't help but smile as they looked at it.

'Wow, so pretty... I love it. And I like the clean, simple style of dress. Although maybe something more showy is better?'

'Who can say? Not me...'

'Aww, would it kill you to show a little interest? These dresses emphasise the line of your body, though. I'd have to go on a diet for sure...'

Ken gave Ryoko a cool murmur in reply as he unfolded the stationery. The letter was written in blue ink, and the bright colour brought to mind the colour of the sea of the far-off town where Kotomi was living.

Dear Takarada-san,

Thank you for your help surrounding the wedding plans. Thanks to you, the ceremony went off without a hitch. I'm so grateful.

The way my parents' relationship has changed over the past few years was making me nervous, and I wasn't sure if I should leave them to go overseas, but they seem to have rallied.

Thank you so much for lending a gentle ear to all the anxieties that I shed like tears when we met and taking the history of my family into account to give such apt advice. Without your help, I don't think my family would have been able to hold together. Thank you so much.

During the ceremony, my dad seemed so nervous, but he was able to give a lovely address at the end. He was sort of awkward and faltered a bit, but I felt so happy to be born as his daughter.

When I told him how great his speech was, he said, 'It's thanks to Takarada-san and your mother,' with a smile. And he said to give you his regards.

Really, I would have liked to stop by and extend my gratitude directly, but unfortunately that's not possible. I'm not sure when it will be, but next time I'm in Japan, I'll be sure to stop by. Looking forward to seeing you.

Kotomi

Ken put the letter back into the envelope and murmured, 'I wish you much happiness.'

'Huh? What's that about?!' asked Ryoko.

'Never mind.'

Time continued to pass slowly at the stationery shop Shihodo in Tokyo's Ginza.

Scissors

'Hey, Haruna. Could you take care of this for me?'

Suzuka thrust the broom into my hands.

'Huh? Why? It's not my day . . .'

'We have an important errand to run. The ones with acrylic standees are limited edition, you know, so, please and thank you.'

The girls in Suzuka's group shuffled backwards in a cluster as they all thanked me in advance with pleading gestures. Once they were out of the classroom, they ran down the hall. As their footsteps receded, I heard someone say, 'Are you sure she won't tell the teacher?' and then someone else reply, 'Nah, we're good.'

I sighed, stood the broom against the podium and began moving all the desks to the back of the room. *Does this count as bullying?* I wondered. It wasn't as if they ignored me or physically attacked me, but whenever something felt like a pain to them, they made me do it. I know part of the problem is my personality that doesn't allow me to refuse when someone makes a request, but I'm not sure what to do about it.

How did it all start . . .? Maybe it was that time before the summer holidays when I said the wrong thing when the topic of 'favourite idols' came up.

Everyone was talking excitedly about Johnnys, LDH or their favourite Korean pop stars, and when the question was suddenly posed to me . . . 'What about you, Haruna? Who do you like?'

'Umm . . . Kenji Miyazawa, Chuya Nakahara . . .'

Notes from the Ginza Shihodo Stationery Shop

I got caught so off guard that I said the names of my favourite poets. I immediately regretted not thinking for a second and mentioning the name of an idol group I knew. Of course, if I had done that, they might have dug in to ask my *oshi*, or my favourite song... So, in the end, maybe it was better that I didn't lie.

After that, they must have looked it up online or something. Every so often, someone says, 'You're all *yuyaaaaan yuyooooon, yuya yuyon*, right, Haruna?' teasing me with a line from Chuya's 'Circus'.

It's not as if I want to be part of their group. On the contrary, I wish they'd leave me alone. From my perspective, all my classmates are such children – why would I want to talk to them? I don't want to make my parents worry, so I go to school, but really, I want to escape as soon as possible.

I want to grow up as fast as I can so I can get a job, use the money I make to buy as many books and writing materials as I want and lead the kind of life where I can have a quiet cup of tea with adult friends who won't make fun of Kenji or Chuya.

Oh right, tomorrow is our job-shadowing field trip. I didn't know who I would be paired with, but I'd get to experience what it's like to work at this stationery shop I love, Shihodo. Looking forward to that, I bottled up the urge to scream and set about doing the cleaning I'd had thrust upon me.

'Hey, Haruna.' Mihashi-kun took his bag off his shoulder as he called to me. I sighed in spite of myself. Our teacher had said they were deciding who else would go, so I should just meet them on site. I never thought it would be Mihashi-kun.

Mihashi-kun and I ended up in the same class for the first time this year. He's the football team's ace – good enough to be chosen for the Tokyo select team. Tall and outstandingly athletic, he's massively popular with all the girls. He's also the type who can get along with anyone, always the centre of whatever group he's in – from my perspective, he's overwhelming, and I would have rather not have been put with him.

'So this is Shihodo? I've never been.'

'What?' In my head, I couldn't help but shoot back, *You've never been, but you chose it as your job-shadowing assignment?*

'I mean, you can buy notebooks and pens and stuff at the newsagent's or a 100-yen shop. And if they don't have something, you can order it online. Does anyone go out of their way to go to a stationery shop these days?'

'I . . . see.'

There was no getting through to him. Of course, even I buy stuff at convenience stores. But when I'm buying something I'll be using for a while or I want something cute, I definitely want to go to a stationery shop with a decent selection. And even if you don't plan on buying anything, it's fun just looking around the shop. I stop by Shihodo at least once a week for that reason.

We stood side by side next to the cylindrical postbox gazing at the entrance to the shop. As we were absent-mindedly staring at ourselves in our school uniforms reflected in the well-polished glass doors, a man came out from inside and practically glided over to us.

'Good morning.'

I hurriedly took my bag off my shoulder and bowed my head. 'G-good morning.'

Mihashi-kun chimed in on just the 'morning' part as he bobbed his head.

'Eita Mihashi-san and Haruna Tagawa-san, correct? I've

been expecting you. Oh, but if we get into a discussion here, we'll be in the way of the other people walking, so we can't take our time. Please come inside.' The man gestured with all his fingers neatly aligned. 'After you.'

'Thanks. C'mon, let's go in.'

At times like this, Mihashi-kun is completely fearless.

'Come on in, Tagawa-san.'

I stepped inside on the man's urging.

'Wow, it's so big! The ceiling is so high we could practically play badminton, don't you think, Haruna?'

'Uh, yeah . . .'

Really, I wanted to tell him not to talk so loud; though, of course, I couldn't say it.

From behind us, the man chuckled at our exchange. He always has a gentle smile on his face and speaks in a relaxed tone. He wears a light blue shirt with a plain navy tie, grey slacks, black leather shoes – always the same look all year round. Though he does sometimes wear a cardigan when it's cold.

Even with someone like me who only ever spends a few hundred yen on a highlighter, a notebook, a stationery set or whatnot, he's polite, and he always gives shiny brand-new coins as change.

'So, I'm Ken Takarada, the manager of Shihodo Stationery.'

Surprisingly, the man – or rather, Takarada-san – handed us each a business card. It was a simple card featuring the shop name and Takarada-san's name, plus the address and email address, but it was really cool and elegant.

'You read this as "Ken"? It's the same *kanji* as *suzuri* – inkstone, right?' said Mihashi-kun as he looked at the card. *I wish I could chat so casually.*

'Yes, you're right, Mihashi-kun.'

'It's a very stationery shop name, huh? Oh, and you can call me Eita. All the adults I know call me that. And please stop with the *keigo*. We're not customers, so you don't have to be so formal.'

Mihashi-kun was ever himself. Really, I wanted to tug his sleeve and say, 'Hey, don't be rude,' but it was all I could do to just stand there.

Takarada-san's face went blank for a moment, but he was smiling again right away. 'Oh, excuse me. It gives me hope to see that the kids at my alma mater have their act together. Ah, I know I come off formal, but at work, that's just how I talk. Also, it might be old-fashioned, but I think it would be awfully impolite to call you by your given name before we get to know each other better.'

Takarada-san had to be a lot older than us, but his slightly troubled frown was adorable.

Mihashi-kun shook his head. 'At our middle school, and at the elementary school I graduated from, being called by our given names is the norm. If anything, they add -san to that. Right, Haruna?'

'Y-yeah . . .'

Actually, I didn't think it was true. But I didn't think it was worth disagreeing with.

Takarada-san said, 'Is that right?' in surprise.

'I mean, your family name can change on the whims of your parents. And some kids have parents from another country, so their family names are hard to pronounce, or awkward to use – some countries don't even have family names! So lots of teachers these days call kids by their given names.'

'I see! I'm learning a lot.'

Mihashi-kun nodded. 'Of course, I'm sure there's regional

variation, but the teachers I've come into contact with have all been that way. Also, since we're here for job shadowing, you're our boss now, if only for a day. You can just call me plain Eita,' said Mihashi-kun as he put the business card in the pocket of his blazer. *If you put it directly into your pocket, it could get bent or warped*, I thought as I slipped mine into the student handbook I kept in my pocket.

'I see . . . Well then, just for today I'll call you Eita-san and Haruna-san. In exchange, please call me Ken-san.'

'Ken-san . . . Sounds so cool, somehow. Got it!' Mihashi-kun grinned, showing his gleaming white teeth.

'First, let's go to the storage area on the first floor.'

We followed Ken-san to the back of the shop where there was a staircase. Since the shop wasn't open yet, most of the lights weren't on, so it was easy to see how much light streamed in through the windows.

Usually, there was a sign that said, 'WORKSHOP IN PROGRESS!' or 'TODAY'S WORKSHOPS HAVE ENDED', placed there to restrict customers from going up, but today it was standing off to the side. Partway up the stairs was a pretty spacious landing with a good view of the shop below.

It was years ago now, but I'd participated in a craft workshop here, so I'd got this view just once before. The same little table and chairs were on the landing.

'Nice . . .' said Mihashi-kun as he dropped into a chair with zero hesitation and peered out over the floor between the railing posts.

'Ah, err, shouldn't you get permission to sit here?'

It was rare for me to say what I was thinking like that, but that's how shocked I was.

'No, feel free. Haruna-san, you can sit, too.' Ken-san pulled out the chair opposite Mihashi-kun for me.

'Are you sure?'

'Of course. Actually, one of the regulars who has been coming here for decades loves to sit up here with a cup of coffee. He can sit up here absent-mindedly gazing out over the floor for an hour at a time. I'm always anxious about something, so I can't sit still for more than five minutes.'

'I see what you mean. I'm good, too. We're headed up this way, right?' Mihashi-kun hopped to his feet and continued up the stairs without waiting for Ken-san. *But he only just let us sit here...*

Ken-san must have read my expression, because he gave me a little nod.

'You can take your time another day, Haruna-san. After all, you're a regular, too.'

'Huh?'

'You come a few times a month, right? I seem to recall that you often buy pens and stationery. Oh, and at the start of the year, you purchased a fountain pen.'

I was surprised. I never imagined he would remember me.

I used my New Year's money this year to splurge on a fountain pen – at Shihodo. Ken-san had given me advice about all different things for nearly an hour.

'This is Pilot's Custom 742, which has a wide variety of nib options. In addition to the six basic types, there are three for a softer touch, and seven specialised types, making a total of sixteen. Do try them all and choose the one that feels most natural for you.'

Then he explained the nibs one at a time and had me

try writing with them. He watched me closely as I wrote, and when I handed him one and said, 'This feels pretty easy to write with,' he nodded.

'The medium, huh? You hold the pen fairly upright, so I think it's a good choice. If you want to use it to write small characters in an organiser, I'd recommend a fine or fine medium, but if you're going to use it to write slightly bigger characters in a notebook or in letters, then the medium should be good.'

I'd never evaluated my options so seriously before buying something, and it was the first time I went to a shop where the staff assisted me so comprehensively, so I remember very well what a thrill it was.

On the first floor, I set my backpack on the slightly raised tatami area, pinned the armband from school that said 'job shadowing' on the left sleeve of my uniform and went back downstairs with Mihashi-kun.

Ken-san had gone down ahead of us and was standing in the bit of open space in front of the till holding a tablet.

'First, I must confess that I usually work alone, so I've never actually done any of the things we're about to do.' Ken-san seemed to have relaxed a bit from earlier.

'What are we about to do?' asked Mihashi-kun.

'Well, I figured we'd start with some radio calisthenics and then have a morning meeting. If we jumped straight into work, I felt like you might struggle to write the report you have to turn in . . .'

'I'm all for radio calisthenics, but we don't need a meeting, do we? Before moving around, it's good to stretch and whatnot – you know, warm up. That's why I think radio calisthenics is a

Scissors

good idea. A meeting will only make us sleepy, so I'm against it.' Mihashi-kun gave his opinion in an easy-going tone, and Ken-san nodded firmly.

'Then let's do that. I suppose I should say I'm relieved. I was stressed about having to say something instructive or give a morning address or what have you.'

We all looked at each other without really meaning to and laughed.

'OK, let's start with the radio calisthenics.'

With that announcement, Ken-san did something on his tablet. Before long, the familiar melody began to play.

'It's so strange . . . How many years has it been? Definitely so long that I have to wonder, yet my body remembers how it goes,' said Ken-san as he swung his arms.

'How long has it been?' asked Mihashi-kun, bending to a surprising depth. Even just by watching him do radio calisthenics, you could tell he was the most athletic kid at school. I *am* on the badminton team but not good enough for them to let me play in any matches, so you can see how different we are.

'Hmm, before I came back here I was working for a hotel and we did them every morning, which means the last time was probably about . . . ten years ago?'

'Wow . . .' My voice and Mihashi-kun's overlapped. *I see, maybe adults get to know each other chatting about nothing in particular during these simple exercises.*

'Oh, um . . . Why did you decide to accept job-shadowers this year?' I managed to get myself to ask.

Ken-san nodded as he took the final deep breath. 'Right, there had been requests in previous years, but there were a lot of businesses around, so I figured there would be enough slots open

Notes from the Ginza Shihodo Stationery Shop

even if I didn't offer any. But these days there are fewer privately run establishments in Ginza, and more places are closing due to the lack of a successor. When I heard that, as a result, there were fewer businesses accepting kids, I felt, especially as a graduate, that it was my duty to participate. Of course, I'm sure the big department stores and restaurants accept lots of students, but in that case, everyone has more or less the same experience, right? So I thought it would be nice to have people experience a small business like this too. Though it's a little embarrassing at the same time . . .'

It was about four months ago that the sheet to request places to job-shadow was handed out. When I saw 'small business – Shihodo Stationery' listed among the usual police and fire departments, train stations, hospitals, department stores, delivery centres, daycares, restaurants and so on, I couldn't help but shriek, 'What!' I was that happy.

'That said, I heard from the teachers that almost no one applied . . . If both of you hadn't applied, I wouldn't have got my two shadowers. I was so nervous!'

That surprised me. I couldn't believe Shihodo was so unpopular.

'Ah, I didn't actually apply. I forgot to turn in the sheet, so our teacher said, "You've been assigned to Shihodo!"'

You didn't have to say that to Ken-san . . . I thought and shot a glare at Mihashi-kun.

'Oh, yeah . . . I wonder what it is. Does the name sound too old-fashioned?'

'Shihodo does sound kind of stuffy!'

After Mihashi-kun said that, I couldn't help but speak up. 'That's not true! I love the name Shihodo! I'm pretty sure it refers to *bunboshiho*, right? The four writing tools. I like the sense of history, and I think it's very Ginza, in a good way! Everyone just wants to go to the same place as their friends, so they apply for places with lots of slots. Or they enjoy spending time with kids, so they want to go to a daycare, or they pick a restaurant that will feed them a tasty staff lunch . . . Oh, and since the reports written by previous students are in the library, I think lots of kids look at those and pick based on them. So . . . I think that . . . next year you'll have way more applicants!'

Mihashi-kun's eyes went wide. 'I don't think I've ever seen you get so fired up about something, Haruna.'

'Ah, it's not . . . a big deal . . .'

Suddenly, I felt embarrassed. But he was right. *What's with me today?*

'Thank you. I'm really glad you two came. Eita-san, you tell me your candid opinion, and Haruna-san, you really value the shop. I can't think of any pair I'd rather have as Shihodo's first student job-shadowers,' Ken-san said with an emphatic nod. *How kind of him.*

'It's almost like we ended up having a morning meeting after all,' laughed Mihashi-kun, and Ken-san murmured, 'True.'

I'd never met an adult who was so nice but also interacted with me as a person rather than treating me like a child. There were teachers and badminton coaches around Ken-san's age, but they all just said their piece or scolded, never actually paying attention to me.

'All right, let's get started. Right this way, please.'

We followed Ken-san. I'd been to the shop so many times, but coming to work – even just job shadowing – instead of as a customer gave me a bit of a different perspective.

Notes from the Ginza Shihodo Stationery Shop

The display shelves were all neatly cleaned; I couldn't spot so much as a speck of dust. Maybe he straightened the products at the end of the day? They were all facing forward in neat columns, with handwritten tags at the front that said the name of the product and the price.

Mihashi-kun must have noticed where I was looking as he came up behind me, because he bent his big frame to move his face closer to one of the display shelves.

'You write each of them by hand, huh? I thought for sure it was just printed to look like handwriting.'

'Yes, after a process of trial and error, I have arrived at handwriting the price tags. At first, I used stamps to make labels that just had the prices, but as customers picked things up and items' positions shifted, I lost track of which prices were for which product . . . After that happened a few times, I started letter-pressing labels that had the names and prices, but none of the fonts I used felt quite right . . . In the end, I concluded that writing the labels out neatly by hand was best. Oh, and the paper, ink, size of the characters, thickness of the lines and whatnot are all the results of experimentation.'

'Huh, but it's weird. The labels of the things that interest you pop right out, while the other ones don't get in the way. Is that because they're handwritten?'

That's what I wanted to say! I screamed in my head, while nodding slightly to agree with Mihashi-kun.

'Hearing you say that makes it feel like the effort is worthwhile. When I go as a customer to other stores, I always find myself examining how products are displayed and labelled. That goes for stationery shops, of course, but also shops that sell clothing or books, and even restaurants and bars. Wherever I go,

Scissors

I'm always looking at those details. Sometimes a close friend of mine gets annoyed and asks, "Can't you just go shopping like a normal person?"

As we were having this conversation, we had come to an area of the sales floor near the big window facing the street. There was a counter the size of a kitchen table, and on the side where it met the shelves behind it was a board a metre across that said in large characters, *We've got your autumn events covered!*

'Now then, the task I'd like to assign to you two is refreshing this special display.'

'Refreshing this special display?' My voice and Mihashi-kun's overlapped.

Ken-san nodded emphatically and explained as he paced back and forth in front of the display. 'Special displays are . . . special. Incidentally, other displays are called regular displays. Regular displays feature designated products in designated locations – for at least six months, once I've decided to stock an item.'

'Ohhh, I see,' Mihashi-kun responded casually.

'Right, and then the special displays get refreshed with different products about once a month. At Shihodo, we have three of them, but this is the largest. It's highly visible from the entrance and brightly lit since it faces the street, so lots of customers stop to check it out. It's not an exaggeration to say that what's displayed here has a major effect on sales for the month.'

'. . . Are you sure it's OK for us to help with such an important display?' I asked anxiously.

'I don't want you to "help". I want to have you handle it,' said Ken-san, his lips turning up in a gentle smile.

'Huh?'

'I want you two to come up with a new display.'

Notes from the Ginza Shihodo Stationery Shop

Mihashi-kun and I looked at each other.

Ken-san continued, unconcerned, 'First, I'll have you choose the products in the shop that you think should go here. You can decide based on some kind of theme or simply round up things you like. Then, please think of a way to display the products that makes them seem even more appealing. I'd also like you to create promotional materials, a poster board and some attention-grabbing signs.'

'You mean like POP ads?' Mihashi-kun chimed in. The way he used a word I'd never heard before made him seem kind of cool.

'Oh, you know your stuff! Yes, POP is an acronym for point of purchase. You can pronounce it like "pop" as you did, or in the retail industry, "P-O-P" will probably be understood as well. POP ads alert customers to what is special about the products and are said to be a powerful sales promotion tool. I hope you'll come up with some that will cause customers to stop in their tracks and pick up a product.'

Mihashi-kun and I exchanged another look. His face said, *Is he serious?*

'Um, how much time do we have?'

'As long as you finish by the end of the day, you're fine. Oh, and I heard you get lunch break from 12 to 1. So please do rest for that hour. I also need to give you thirty minutes to write your report before you leave. So if we say you finish by 4:30, then adding the morning and afternoon time together, you have about six hours.'

'Six hours...' My voice and Mihashi-kun's overlapped again. But what we said after that was completely different.

'If we have that long, it'll be a cinch!'

'That's all . . .?'

Mihashi-kun's confident voice drowned out my murmur.

Ken-san nodded deeply. 'Once you have an idea of what sort of display you'd like to make, I think the actual work will only take two or three hours. The main task is to choose the products and decide a concept for the display. Incidentally, until yesterday, the theme for this display was, as the board says, autumn events. So, basically, you two can do whatever kind of display you want, but please make sure it doesn't overlap with this.'

As Ken-san had explained, the display was filled with writing materials and other products that could be used for autumn events and occasions, such as school culture festivals and sports days, social studies field trips, plus the equinox, viewing autumnal colours and so on. The products all had a POP ad about the size of a business card, each featuring a neatly written explanation of the product's qualities and little illustrations suggesting situations where the product might be handy.

'So we have to clear away all these products and then think about what to put here instead, right?' I asked, looking down at my watch. This was no time to stand around chatting. We'd already lost nearly five minutes.

'No, I'll put away these products now. That should be done in less than thirty minutes. While I do that, I'd like you two to think about what you'd like to put on display. Or, actually, it might make more sense for you to look around the shop and see what kind of products we have first. Of course, you know very well what we carry, Haruna-san, so you may not need to do that . . . Anyhow, you two can decide together how to split up your time. I'll let you know when it's time for lunch. Do you have any questions?'

Mihashi-kun raised his hand. 'I do!'

Notes from the Ginza Shihodo Stationery Shop

'Eita-san.' Ken-san called on him like a teacher would.

'What time does the shop open?'

'Ten o'clock.'

Mihashi-kun nodded at the straightforward response and followed up with another question. 'What should we do if a customer asks us something?'

'Please call me right away. Customer service is quite difficult, so I'm not planning on having you two do any of that.'

'Phew . . . I wasn't sure what I would do if someone asked something tricky. But we can't call you Ken-san in front of the customers, right?'

'Don't worry. You can just shout something like, "Customer service, please!" and I'll come flying over.'

'Somehow when you say it, I feel like you might actually fly.'

The way they were talking made them seem like a young uncle and his nephew, or cousins with an age gap. Somehow I felt left out – not a great feeling.

'OK. Let's get started!' shouted Mihashi-kun, but Ken-san said, 'Just a moment.' He opened a drawer in the special display counter, took out two pairs of brand-new gloves with anti-slip texturing and handed one to each of us.

'Not to be demanding, but when handling products, please use these gloves.'

'Is that so our fingerprints don't get all over the merchandise?' Mihashi-kun asked as he put the gloves on.

'That's one reason, but the main one is that paper can cut your hands. Or you might bump your hand against the edge of a shelf. Gloves protect you from all those accidents.'

At some point when I wasn't looking, Ken-san's hands had been enveloped in the same type of gloves.

'I always make sure to wear gloves when doing this sort of work, too. Working with bare hands, I've sliced myself open on the edge of a cardboard box or the cover of a notepad . . . It's a different kind of pain from cutting yourself with a knife, and those cuts can take a surprisingly long time to heal, so it's annoying. Please do be careful. But OK, go ahead and get started. I'm happy to have you here today.'

'OK, thanks!' For the first time, my voice and Mihashi-kun's aligned in perfect unison. With a firm nod to us, Ken-san began clearing away the autumn event display products.

His brisk movements were so efficient that even though he was just working, I felt as though I were watching a dance or a magic trick. If I could have, I would have watched the whole process.

'Hey, Haruna. Earth to Haruna.' Mihashi-kun's voice brought me back to myself.

'Huh? Oh, err, yeah, what is it?'

'Not "what is it?" You're the one who was all freaked out that we only have six hours, so why are you spacing out? What's our plan?'

'Our plan? You're the one who said it'd be a cinch, so you must have an idea, right?'

Mihashi-kun glanced around the shop.

'How would I have an idea? I've never even been to this place before. Oh, and could you quit with the "Mihashi-kun" thing? This cram school teacher I hated would always call me that, so it brings up bad memories. Just call me Eita. Anyway, you come here a lot, don't you, Haruna?'

'Well, yeah, but . . . not enough to be able to give someone recommendations on what to buy.'

Notes from the Ginza Shihodo Stationery Shop

Mihashi-kun gave me an *Aw, man* kind of look for a second. When I saw his face, I couldn't help but sigh. *This guy has no idea what an uproar it would cause if the other girls saw me calling him 'just Eita' as if we're best friends. But there's no one else around today. If he can call me Haruna, then I can call him Eita.*

Eita grabbed one of the shopping baskets from the corner of the aisle.

'Well, whatever. For now, let's take a spin around the shop. We can see what they have. Um, Ken-san, can we use this basket? I was thinking we could use it to gather the products we want to display.'

'Of course. If one isn't enough, feel free to use two or three – as many as you need.'

With Ken-san's warm gaze on my back, I followed after Eita.

In the end, it took over an hour just to go around the shop and pick out products that caught our eye. The shop had opened on time, and a handful of customers had immediately started trickling in. With a glance at Ken-san busily working the till, we returned to the special display area to find all the previously displayed products cleared away and a sign that said 'coming soon' with a cat and rabbit bowing with apologetic expressions on their faces.

'OK, now what?' Eita looked at me as he set the baskets of products on the counter.

'How am I supposed to . . .?' As I trailed off, Ken-san popped over. He'd only just been working at the till. *How is he so fast?*

'What a plentiful harvest! And here I was worried you'd decide there was nothing that really caught your eye.'

'That would neeever happen!' Eita reacted theatrically.

Scissors

I was kind of annoyed at him as I said, 'But what should we do now? We can't just lay them all out here.'

Ken-san nodded and pointed up at the ceiling. 'Then let's go to the first floor. If you think about how you want to display them and get ready up there, you can take your time and won't get in the way of any customers.'

Once we were upstairs, Ken-san put our baskets on the raised area and gestured to the nearest table. There were six large worktables on big casters arranged in a rectangle.

'For now, lay out the items you selected here.'

Eita and I each took a basket and put all the products on one of the tables. While we did that, Ken-san arranged a couple other tables into a mock-up of the special event space.

'OK, you're all set. By the way, did you decide on a concept for the display?'

Eita and I glanced at each other. How many times did that make today?

'I was wondering about that . . . Or, like, I just picked out things I wanted . . .' I didn't really answer the question, and then Eita chimed in.

'To be honest, I was just surprised how many things you have, including a bunch that made me wonder who on earth would buy them. Do you have a lot of products where you try stocking them and then no one buys a single one?'

Like usual, Eita said exactly what was on his mind, but I was getting used to it.

'You hit me where it hurts, ha. Of course, there are some items that may only sell one in an entire year. But when someone comes in desperate to find something, I'd like to be able to hand it to them on the spot. This is Ginza, after all, so many customers come in needing something right away for work.'

'You're too nice!' jabbed Eita before saying, 'If you were a shop that took job-shadowers every year, we could ask what the kids from the previous year did, but we're the first batch, huh . . .'

This comment from Eita made Ken-san smile.

'Unfortunately, I'm a bit of a contrarian, so I don't think I would have told you even if there had been kids last year. The fun of designing sales displays is coming up with something on your own from scratch. Also, I'd like to see what second-year middle-schoolers will come up with. I'm sure it's a tough assignment, but please see it through.'

'Hmm, I get what you're saying, but . . . what we do will end up being the standard . . . like, for the kids who shadow here in the future . . .' Eita grumbled, but Ken-san shook his head vigorously.

'Please don't give it that much weight. And if there's anything bothering me when you're done, I'll make some revisions.'

'Really? Hmm, well, I guess we just have to give it a shot. But, Ken-san, what sorts of things do you usually consider when designing a display?'

Oh, if we want hints, we can just ask. I didn't think of it till I heard Eita's question.

'Hmm . . . Well, as you pointed out, Shihodo carries all sorts of products, so I often try to highlight products that people might not come in looking for specifically, like, "We have these, too!"'

'I see . . .' My voice and Eita's overlapped again.

'But what about limiting your selection a bit more? I get that you carry a lot of things for the people who want stuff right away, but . . . when you have such a huge selection, I think it actually makes it hard to choose.'

When Eita said that, I shook my head. 'I don't *not* get what you're saying, but . . . I like being able to actually hold different products in my hands and check them out before I buy something.'

I was sort of surprised to find myself giving my opinion. Eita glanced at me.

'These days, you can see pictures and even videos of people using the items in some cases, so I think you can check stuff out without actually holding it in your hand . . .'

We're the same age, yet our way of thinking is completely different.

'Umm . . . I think that might be because you're good at everything, Mihashi-kun – err, Eita. I'm clumsy, so there have been plenty of times when I bought something, only to be disappointed because I wasn't able to use it very well . . .'

'What do you mean? Oh, you're a leftie, huh, Haruna?'

That wasn't the only issue, and his carefree way of responding bothered me. 'Well . . .'

Eita watched my face closely.

'Seems like there's something you wanna say. You can tell me what makes it hard.'

When Eita said that, I felt like I could tell him how I really felt. When I glanced at Ken-san, I saw he was following our conversation with interest.

'. . . Hmm, for example, scissors.'

'Scissors? Oh yeah. There were left-handed scissors in that section downstairs. You picked up a pair, right?'

Sometimes Eita mixes English into his Japanese – like using the verb 'pick up'. He's never even lived overseas, but his pronunciation is so good that the native-speaker teacher always praises him. 'I mean, I want to play in the pro leagues overseas in the future, so of course I have to be able to speak English,' he says like it's no big deal.

'These, right?' Ken-san grabbed the left-handed scissors off the worktable.

'Yeah, those are the ones.'

Eita nodded, and Ken-san began taking the scissors out of their packaging.

'Huh? E-err . . .'

Noting my yelp, Ken-san said, 'Don't worry,' with a smile. 'I was thinking of putting a pair on display as a sample. Now, Eita-san, try holding these in your right hand and cutting something. Oh, one second.'

Ken-san handed the scissors to Eita and then went over to the drawers across from the raised area, took out a piece of paper and then wrote something on it at the old desk in the back.

'Sorry to keep you waiting.' He'd drawn a wavy line on the paper in pencil. 'Please cut along this line.'

Eita began cutting the paper as instructed.

'Huh?'

After cutting just a little bit, the paper collapsed and bent.

'No need to rush. Take your time.'

Nodding at Ken-san's voice, Eita tried cutting again. The two blades slowly sandwiched the paper.

'Err? Nnngh, this is hard.'

It seemed like he was trying to follow the line, but he missed.

'It's pretty difficult, right? Let me see.'

I took the scissors from Eita, held them in my left hand, and cut effortlessly through the paper.

Scissors

'Well, you're left-handed, so it makes sense that you'd be able to do it.' His tone was full-on sore loser. 'But what makes left-handed scissors different from regular scissors?' he asked, his eyes fixed on the scissors I'd returned to the worktable.

'I don't really appreciate that phrasing. "Regular scissors" makes it sound like there's something irregular about left-handed scissors.' I'd said it before I even realised. The strength of my voice surprised me.

'It's just a figure of speech. Uhh, so what's the difference between right-handed scissors and left-handed scissors?'

After Eita rephrased, Ken-san nodded. 'One moment, please.' He went back to the old desk, opened a drawer and took out another pair of scissors. 'These are right-handed. And here are the left-handed ones you just tried to cut with. Can you tell how they're different?'

The two pairs of scissors on the table were from the same brand, so at a glance it was hard to see any difference.

Eita picked them up and pondered the question. 'Hrm . . .'

'These are both Fitcut Curve standard models with antibacterial grips from Plus. They're just the right size for general use and have an enduring popularity, including here at Shihodo.'

'Oh!' Eita said suddenly. Maybe he hadn't been listening to Ken-san at all. 'I got it. The top and bottom blades are swapped!'

'Yes, that's exactly right.' Ken-san nodded emphatically and picked up the right-handed scissors as he began his explanation. 'As you've noticed, scissors cut things by sandwiching them between a top and bottom blade. Scissors have two finger holes. The blade attached to the hole where your thumb goes is the dynamic blade, while the other is known as the static blade. These two blades cross at a specific angle. Where they meet is called the contact point. It's at the contact point that the target object is pressed between the blades and cut. This screw connecting the dynamic and static blades is called the pivot screw, but if you remove it and try to cut paper by pressing one of the blades against it, you can't. Scissors can only cut when the two blades come together at one point.'

'Ohhh...' Eita and I both emitted a dopey reaction. I'd never thought about how scissors cut something before.

'Right-handed scissors are designed so the force of your hand is brought to bear on the contact point when you grip them with your right hand. When a left-handed person uses them, due to the structure of human hands, the force escapes. That's why unless you get used to them, it's very hard to cut things with right-handed scissors as a left-handed person.'

'Huh, I never knew that,' said Eita, impressed.

'Incidentally, say a right-handed person is cutting with a pair of right-handed scissors. In this case, the palm of the hand naturally faces to the left, so watching the contact point from the left makes it easy to cut. When a left-handed person uses right-handed scissors, the palm of their hand faces right, but they have to watch the contact point on the other side. Most of the time, you hold the paper, fabric or whatnot that you're cutting from the side opposite the cutting hand. Working across your body's central line must be tiring.'

Eita gripped each of the scissors in turn as he finished listening to Ken-san's explanation. 'Oh... This is tough,' he said, glancing at me.

'... Yeah.'

'All the scissors at school are right-handed, right? I mean, you might have your own pair of left-handed scissors, but . . . What do you do when you suddenly need scissors in the library or the art room or wherever?'

I sensed that Eita's voice had grown just a little softer.

'Well, if it's just something quick, I use the right-handed scissors. And my grandma always trained me, like, "Use your right hand!" so I can use chopsticks and write and whatnot with my right hand.'

'But you're a leftie in badminton, right?'

I was kind of surprised that he knew what I was like during badminton. I kept my answer clipped to not betray how flustered I was. 'Y-yep . . .'

Eita looked between the two pairs of scissors once again.

'You're good at everything, Mihashi-ku – err, Eita, so you probably never imagined that it might be hard for someone to use these kinds of everyday tools, huh?'

'I don't think I'm good at "everything" . . . Oh, a minute ago you were saying there were times you were disappointed because you were too clumsy to use the stuff you bought well. Are there other examples?'

I looked up at Eita, who is a whole head taller than me. 'I'm pretty small, right? That might have something to do with the fact that my grip and arms in general are weaker than other people's. Sometimes things that seem easy for other people to do are hard for me.'

'Hmm, like what?'

'I mean, I can't think of anything off the top of my head, but . . . Oh! Remember when we had to write a report about our social studies field trip on butcher paper in our groups? I couldn't get the cap off the permanent marker. In the end,

Notes from the Ginza Shihodo Stationery Shop

Yamada-kun opened it for me . . . Oh, and I'm also bad at using tape dispensers. I can never figure out how much force to use, so I end up pulling too hard, and then the tape is too long. And I'm not good at cutting it against the teeth on the dispenser, so sometimes it gets messed up. Honestly, I think making good use of all these items takes skill.'

I wasn't sure why – maybe because Eita was kindly focused on me, nodding now and then as he listened – but I was able to say everything I wanted to.

Ken-san, who had been listening to our conversation, quietly made a note.

'Oh, did we say something weird?' Eita asked abruptly.

'Oh, no, not at all. Nothing weird. On the contrary, I thought you were having an excellent discussion, so I took a note. It's very instructive. Adults, including me, always use how busy we are as an excuse to say, "This is just how it is," and carry on without really thinking, but you two are having a great exchange of viewpoints.'

Eita laughed self-consciously. 'Heh-heh.'

'Err . . . do you mean that? You aren't just trying to find any way to compliment us?' I mustered the will to ask.

'No, I really thought it was good.'

'So, then . . . it wouldn't be weird to have a display of products that are easy to use for everyone, would it?'

'Ohhh . . . That sounds interesting.'

But Eita cocked his head. 'But is there enough stuff to fill all that space?'

'There is. I mean, I think so . . .'

He fixed his eyes on me before nodding emphatically. 'Then it's settled! Ken-san, can we go and reselect our items?'

'Of course.' Ken-san smiled with a deep nod.

'OK, then let's clean these up for starters.' Eita started putting the products laid out on the table back into the shopping baskets.

'I'll take care of this. You two can go and choose products.'

'No, we brought these here, so we'll put them back. We'll be wandering the sales floor again anyhow, so we can do it while we look around.'

I nodded in agreement with Eita.

Before we knew it, it was noon. While putting back the items we'd picked up in the morning, we went around the entire shop and selected products that would fit our 'easy to use for everyone' theme. If you can believe it, we managed to find three baskets full.

When we took the baskets up, we found that lunch had arrived from a cafe in the neighbourhood. A pretty lady Ken-san had been friends with since childhood who was also a graduate of our middle school, Ryoko-san, had delivered it.

'Ta-da! This is Hohozue's famous *Naporitan*! We prepared an extra-large portion for Eita-kun and a large for Haruna-chan.'

'Wow, cafe Naporitan is my favourite food! Ooh, there's plain greens with just some potato salad and tomato, plus consommé sprinkled with dried parsley – perfect!' said Eita.

'Err, I'm not sure if that's a compliment or a diss, but you seem happy, so I forgive you! Enjoy your lunch!'

'*Itadakimasu*!' Eita had stuck his fork into the ketchup-y pasta before Ryoko-san even finished speaking. 'Yum!' After giving his impression in that single word, he completely absorbed himself in eating.

Notes from the Ginza Shihodo Stationery Shop

'U-umm, if you rush like that, you'll get it on your shirt . . .' I hurried to warn him, and Ryoko-san burst out laughing.

'I still say pretty much the same thing to Ken-chan all the time! And he never changes. Instead he just says stuff like, "I'm actually expressing how tasty it is with my entire body." All boys are like this! They basically stay children forever. Oh, there's iced coffee in the thermos. Feel free to finish off your meal with that. OK, I'm going to watch the shop for Ken-chan, so I'll see you later.'

Ryoko-san practically skipped down the stairs. When I glanced up at Eita across from me, he was battling his pasta, the whole area around his mouth bright red from the sauce. About half of his mountain of spaghetti was already gone.

'It's so good. Eat already!'

'I am.'

In front of me was an oval, stainless-steel plate piled high with Naporitan. It was a simple recipe with sausage, green pepper, onion, carrot – but the sauce had so much depth, it seemed like there must have been some secret ingredients. It was clear from the subtle flavours that the consommé and green salad had also been prepared with care.

'Wow, I'd expect nothing less from a second-year middle-schooler. You seem to be having no trouble with that extra-large.' Ken-san came up from downstairs and took a seat. After wiping his hands on a moist towel, he sat up straight and bowed his head to say, 'Itadakimasu.'

'It's tasty, and there's a lot of it, so this is the best. I'm really glad I chose Shihodo to shadow at!'

Would you listen to that? Did he forget that he confessed to being assigned here automatically after forgetting to turn in his application?

Scissors

'When I'm with you two, I almost feel like I'm back in middle school. It's really a lot of fun.'

We forgot work for a little while and enjoyed lunch as we chatted about what the kids in class are into, what's been happening lately at school and so on.

Maybe it's natural for a customer service professional, but Ken-san is a good listener, so I spoke more than usual. Maybe I could talk to him more easily because he's a grown-up who isn't one of my parents or a teacher.

'OK, now that we've fortified our stomachs, let's get to work on designing that display.'

While Eita and Ken-san cleared away the dishes, I laid out the products we'd chosen near the worktables set up as a mock display area.

When Eita and Ken-san approached after cleaning up, I picked up a pair of scissors with a package that pointed out they were *'For lefties!'*

'Even just counting the tools for left-handed people, there were so many. That's what all these are . . . For example, this box-cutter. I've always just been powering through with right-handed box-cutters! When you think about it, bladed tools are dangerous if you're not using one made for the correct hand . . . If I had realised handy items like this existed, I would have looked harder to find one.'

I really am speaking better today. I don't think I've talked this long with anyone outside my family before.

'Ahh . . .' Ken-san nodded.

'But I noticed that these, uh, cutting mats? – the rubber pads you lay under whatever you're cutting – only come in right-handed versions,' Eita was kind enough to add, and I nodded emphatically.

'That's true, there aren't any left-handed cutting mats,' said Ken-san. 'I did try looking . . . As you noticed, there are grid lines, but the vertical scale is only printed on the left side, and on the horizontal scale, the numbers count up from left to right, so left-handed users have to calculate in reverse.'

'The same goes for rulers. All the scales go from left to right. I can write with my right hand, so I'm not really inconvenienced, but . . . In elementary school, the kids who held their pencils with their left hands always had a hard time in lessons where we used triangles and protractors . . .'

It happened again. The words just came out.

'Ah, I see. Oh, but look: the edge is left to right, but they put small numbers right to left on the inside. Ahh, I guess there's not much they can do about it, but the font is so small. People with weak eyesight might not be able to read them.'

Ken-san took the ruler from Eita. 'Yeah, people with ageing eyes probably won't be able to read them either.'

'Not that you'd have any occasion to use a protractor or triangle at that age. But maybe that's why grown-ups forget how hard it is.'

The way he said it was blunt, but I agreed with Eita.

'More surprising to me was the number of products with packages that say things like, "easy to use with a light touch" or "easy to open with one hand" – like, the idea that you don't need a lot of strength. I didn't realise so many people had trouble with stuff like that.' Eita looked a little embarrassed.

'That's a great thing to notice. Even though I'm the one who stocked these items, I didn't realise there were so many that put an emphasis on the user experience . . . It's a bit of a surprise for me.' Ken-san was looking down at all the products we'd selected.

'This Sakuri Flat stapler from Max uses a double lever to reduce the force needed to staple something by half.'

'Gripping things does take strength,' I said almost without thinking, and Ken-san nodded.

'Yes, supposedly the average grip strength of an adult male is forty-five kilograms. Meanwhile, the average for women is between twenty-five and thirty.'

'They only have about half?' Eita asked, seeming surprised, and Ken-san nodded.

'And the grip strength of men starts to weaken around age fifty and by sixty-five, theirs has fallen to about thirty kilograms as well. Incidentally, a younger elementary schooler has about thirteen and maybe twenty by the time they're in their last year or so.'

'The last time I measured mine, it was fifty!'

'Wow! That's amazing. If you put in some effort and get it to eighty, I heard you'll be able to crush an apple, and then you can sell "real" hand-pressed apple juice.'

'What? Really? OK, I'll do my best.'

I laughed, thinking it was like Ryoko-san had said: maybe guys really do keep middle-school mentality forever.

'Apologies . . . I took us on a tangent. Speaking of levers, the Air Karu clip from Plus doesn't take much strength to open and close, either.' Ken-san opened the package and took one out.

'They just made the levers longer, so that's a pretty simple tweak.' Eita pinched it, impressed.

'They did make the levers longer, but supposedly this little bump they put on the part that closes also has an effect. I heard from someone at the company that they tried a ton of different versions before arriving at this one. Incidentally, it won an excellence award for functionality in the 2018 Nihon Bungu Taisho.'

'Wow, a little item like this could win a big prize like that?'

I knew how Eita felt. The clip suddenly seemed more precious.

'So, for now, we should split these items into groups that have something in common and then figure out a way to lay them out so they look nice?'

Ken-san answered Eita with a nod. 'Yes, as you said, Eita-san, decide how you'll position the products first. Then, as I explained earlier, I'd like you to design some POP ads that will have customers picking up the items before they even realise it.'

He paused there to go into one of the drawers in the wall to bring out two toolboxes.

'Feel free to use the tools and writing utensils in here. There's a wider selection available, so if you need anything, please ask. I can bring you just about anything.'

One of the boxes was actually filled with tools, while the other was packed with all sorts of writing utensils.

'Wow . . .' The sheer number rendered me speechless.

'Your face is like, "A treasure chest of things to write with!" Ken-san, we can really use any of these?'

'Yes, go ahead. Any way you like. These are the pens and whatnot I usually use when creating POP ads, so you don't need to hold back. Oh, and if something is out of ink, don't put it back in the box. Just let me know and I'll bring a replacement. And then there are rolls of butcher paper and kraft paper over here, and I'll put out some styrene boards and construction paper. I think this should be enough, but if there's anything else you want, let me know. As long as I have it in stock downstairs, I can let you use it.'

Scissors

After giving that explanation, Ken-san glanced at his watch.

'It's one thirty, so you have three hours till four thirty. Please work together to create a display that satisfies you! I'll leave you to it.'

Ken-san took the tray with the dishes and went downstairs.

Once he was out of sight, Eita took off his blazer and tie and rolled the sleeves of his shirt up.

'First, let's split the stuff into groups. Uhhh, let's put stuff for lefties over here. And . . . there was a whole bunch of things that you could use with less strength, right?'

He'd seemed like such a child until a moment ago, but now he came off so reliable, somehow. Still, I felt like I couldn't take advantage of that. I had to pull my weight.

'. . . Oh, uh, can I make a suggestion?'

'Huh? What is it? Of course you can. There are only two of us, so you can just say it.'

'Oh, uh, thanks. Why don't we decide on an order of operations before we start? If we don't plan how to divide the labour and use our time to work efficiently, I don't think we'll make it in time . . .'

'I getcha,' said Eita. 'OK, then let's do that. So how about we group the items, decide on the theme for each group and then look at all the group names to come up with the overall title for the display? We can build it up like that. If we decide the overall theme at the start, we'll end up stuck with some products that don't really work.'

I was impressed. He almost never made comments in class and always went rushing outside the moment it was breaktime, so I hadn't realised he was such a quick thinker.

'What do you think? If you disagree, go ahead and say so.

If you don't just say whatever with no filter during the brainstorming phase, you don't end up with any good ideas.'

'Oh, err, I think what you said is good. Let's do that.'

'OK, then I'll make some rough groups. You think of the names for the groups. Doesn't have to be just one. Write whatever you come up with on these sticky notes and stick them on the table. Once everything's split up, we'll review the groups together. Then we'll look at the sticky notes and write stuff big on the board to make our final decisions. Let's get that done in the first hour. After that, we can take an hour to make POP ads and the signboard. The last hour can be for setting up downstairs.'

'Got it.'

I kind of got a feel for why Eita was always the centre around which everything else revolved.

After that, we were able to finish deciding the group names and concept fifteen minutes early, but creating all the POP ads took over an hour and a half. It was about 3:50 by the time we went downstairs to set up.

I did the more detailed positioning, while Eita handled the bigger pieces like the signboard. Sometimes he'd ask for my opinion – 'Do you think this looks OK?' – or say things like, 'Wow, Haruna! That looks awesome! You're a genius!'

I felt like Eita and I were really working as a team to design the special display, and it was the most fulfilling three hours I'd had since starting middle school.

'We did it!'

'Done!'

We both shouted without really meaning to.

Usually I didn't express my emotions so openly, so I wonder

Scissors

what was different. I felt a bit embarrassed. But all our efforts paid off – I think the display we came up with was really good.

'All done?' After seeing a customer off, Ken-san came over to the special display area.

'Yeah, somehow we managed it.' I hurriedly checked my watch. It was exactly 4:30. Somehow, we'd finished in time.

'Ooh, this is great.' Ken-san stood in the aisle with his back to the entrance and looked at the display.

'If there's anything you think needs changing, go right ahead!'

I nodded emphatically to agree with Eita.

'No, the board at the front is just the right size and height. The colours match the atmosphere of the shop, too. No edits necessary.'

'Phew...'

'Yes!'

I was relieved, and Eita pumped a fist.

The signboard at the front – 'Easy to use for everyone! A collection of accessible products' – Eita had made. He'd cut a styrene board into an oval, covered it in cream-coloured paper and painted the words in navy poster paint so dark it almost looked black. His calligraphy was surprisingly, like, good? He'd used a flat brush to do gothic characters.

'The POP ads for the group, as well as the small ones pointing out the strengths of each item, are well done, too. Whose idea was it to change the colour of paper for each group?'

'That was Eita. He suggested we change the colour so that each group would have, like, its own uniform.'

'Heh-heh, yeah, it just came to mind.'

Ken-san nodded at Eita's response and then admired the display from all different angles, moving closer or farther away.

Then he said, 'I'm going to make a couple of adjustments,' before moving certain items to the front or adjusting the sideways distance between items. His tweaks were so slight, but they made the whole thing look even better.

That's the difference between a pro and amateurs, I thought.

He turned to look at us with a nod. 'That should do it. Well done, you two.'

'Woo-hoo!'

'Phew . . .'

Eita put his hands up for a high five, so I gave him one without thinking. It might have been my first high five ever. But in the moment our hands smacked together, I felt like Eita and I really understood each other.

'I don't really know quite how to put it, but you two make a good team. I don't think either of you could have come up with this display on your own. It took both of you working together to create something this lovely.' Ken-san nodded a few times.

'Working together . . . It's kind of like scissors, huh?' Eita murmured. That hadn't occurred to me in the slightest.

'Oh, um . . .'

Just as I was about to speak, a customer came in. Ken-san immediately greeted them with an 'Irasshaimase!' Eita and I chimed in. 'Irasshaimase!'

'Oh my, this place is friendly, I see,' the customer replied happily. Her voice was strong, but she looked to be about the age of my great-grandma, and maybe she had bad knees? She was walking with a cane. She bobbed her head to us and then glanced around. Maybe she was looking for something specific.

In no time, Ken-san was at her side. 'Welcome. Can I help you find something?'

She nodded deeply. 'Yes! I'd like a pair of scissors.'

'Scissors – very well. We have all different kinds over there. Please follow me.'

Ken-san gestured with an open arm, but the customer shook her head.

'Not just any scissors. Umm, they were on TV the other day . . . These scissors that take less strength to cut with. Err, where did it go? I wrote down the name somewhere.' She plunged a hand into her bag and started rummaging around.

'Uh, might these be the ones?'

At some point, Eita had appeared next to Ken-san. In his hands were a pair of scissors we had just put out in our display.

'They're called, uh . . . Rakurakubasami.'

'Yes, yes, these are the ones! These were on TV!' She happily took the scissors from Eita. 'But I wonder if I'll really be able to use them.'

Ken-san nodded and turned to me. 'Haruna-san, would you go and grab another pair of these for me?'

I rushed to grab another pair and then hurried back to where everyone was standing. When I held out the scissors, Ken-san took them out of the package.

'These are from a company called Abilities Carenet. They focus on assistive technology, so these are made with a few special tricks. Give them a try.' Ken-san held out the scissors, along with a little piece of paper from his pocket.

'You don't mind if I cut this?'

'Go ahead.'

Eita and I nodded at Ken-san's reply.

'I'm a little nervous . . .' she said with a laugh as she tried out the scissors. 'Wow, they really are easy to use! What a surprise!'

Eita and I looked at each other with a smile.

'You might be interested in the special display over here. We collected all sorts of easy-to-use products – items for lefties, tools that don't require too much strength and so on.' Eita spoke up in a clear voice to direct her to the special display.

'Please take a look . . . if you like.' I mustered my courage to chime in.

'Wow, there are so many!'

'Yup, err, I mean – indeed,' said Eita. I only came here for the first time today, but yeah, there's all kinds of stuff.'

'Are you two middle-schoolers? With those armbands, you must be getting some work experience?'

'That's right. I wasn't really interested in stationery and stuff, but it's actually pretty interesting. Do you know what this is?'

Eita took the customer over to the display and started showing her all sorts of things. I really envied how he was able to get along with anyone right away.

'Err, hey, Haruna. What was so cool about this thing, again?'

'Oh, that.'

He could just read the POP ad . . . I thought, but then I realised: he was pretending not to know on purpose in order to include me in the discussion with the customer. Before today, I had no idea he was so considerate.

Then the woman listened intently as we explained various things, occasionally responding with a 'Wow!' or 'That's fantastic!' Then she bought seven items.

'Thanks. Now I'll be able to work for a little longer.' She bowed to Eita and me.

'Oh, you don't have to . . .'

This might have been the first time someone thanked me so politely.

'Oh, I said work, but it's not as if I get paid or anything. I just help out at the neighbuorhood association with things like organising paperwork and hanging bulletin-board posts. But things that used to be no trouble for me have been getting harder and harder. I figured if I was only going to get in everyone's way, maybe it would be better to let someone younger take over, but with the items you two showed me today, I'll be all right! I can keep going for a while!'

Cradling the purchases Ken-san had wrapped up for her, the customer left the shop. As we watched her go, Eita murmured, 'It feels kinda good when a customer is happy.'

Ken-san nodded. 'Yes, that's the greatest reward of working at a shop.'

I nodded deeply at his remark. Once she was out of sight, we went back inside.

'Well, that's the end of your workday. Nice job, both of you. Please write your report upstairs.'

On Ken-san's urging, we headed to the first floor. Partway up, on the landing, I turned around to Eita and said, 'Thanks for today.'

Eita looked at me blankly. 'Oh, thank you too, I guess? What's up?'

'You know, I don't fit in at school . . . I realise I should get my act together. But I had fun today. I just figured that since we'll be back in class tomorrow, I wouldn't have the chance to say it . . .'

Eita seemed surprised. 'You don't fit in? Sounds like you're talking about me – 'cause I don't read the room. You get good grades and you're nice to everyone . . . Though I think people take advantage of you 'cause you're too nice. You should be yourself more. You hold back a bit too much. And you gotta tell people what you want to do. You know, you can't score a goal unless you call for a pass.'

The fact that he used a football analogy was very Eita. But his earnest engagement made me happy.

'But, Eita, the ball comes to you even if you don't do that, right?'

Eita shook his head. 'Nope! If you want a pass, the first thing you have to do is pass the ball to someone else. And unless you call for a pass, no one knows you're open. Today you talked to me, right? And you suggested what we should do. You gotta keep that up. Anyhow, let's bang out that report.' With that, he ran up the rest of the stairs.

* * *

A figure in a coat carrying a delivery tray hurried by the swaying willows. It was Ryoko, the poster girl of Hohozue. She entered Shihodo Stationery as if being sucked through the doors.

'Sorry to keep you waiting . . . What's going on today? Three servings of Hayashi rice, and not only that, but one large and one extra-large? All together, I think it's easily enough food for six people. Agh, it's so heavy!'

The manager, Ken Takarada, looked up from behind the counter where he was organising receipts. 'Sure, I see, but I don't think there being a lot is any excuse to be late.'

'. . . Well, I don't have anything to say back to that. Anyhow, where should I set up? Upstairs?'

Scissors

Ken glanced towards the staircase at the back of the shop and nodded. 'Yeah, could you take it upstairs for me? There are customers. Oh, the regular portion you can leave here. I'll inhale it.'

'OK!' As soon as she replied, she laid out Hayashi rice, green salad, consommé and a set of silverware wrapped in a napkin. 'All right. I'll take the rest upstairs.'

'Thanks!'

Ken must have been awfully busy – he continued organising paper slips with his left hand, while with his right he deftly unrolled the napkin and plunged the spoon into the Hayashi rice.

'Ahh, if you don't look where you're eating, you're going to spill it.'

'I'll be fine! Better hurry upstairs. I bet the customers are starving.'

'Yeah, yeah.'

With a sigh, Ryoko picked up the delivery tray and climbed the stairs.

'Excuse me, I'm here with lunch . . . Err? Is that Haruna-chan and Eita-kun?'

The pair who turned around at her voice were Haruna Tagawa and Eita Mihashi in their school uniforms.

'Oh, Ryoko-san!' Haruna and Eita's voices overlapped.

'What are you two doing here? Not more job shadowing, right?' Ryoko set the delivery tray on a worktable.

'No . . . But our report got selected to represent the ward. So we'll participate in the Tokyo Prefecture Work Experience Forum that started this year,' said Haruna bashfully.

'Isn't that amazing? Well, there are only four middle schools in Chuo Ward, so it's one of the easier wards to end up as a rep of, but . . .' Eita laughed as he self-consciously scratched the back of his head.

'You *are* amazing, both of you! Congrats!'

As they chatted, Ryoko took out the Hayashi rice and salad and laid them out on the low table on the raised tatami area.

'Whoa, Hayashi rice! That might be my favourite food in the whole world!'

'I feel like you said something very similar about Naporitan last time . . .'

'Huh? Did I? Well, whatever. Let's fortify our stomachs first. We can think after that.' Glossing over Haruna's murmur, Eita kicked his trainers off and hopped up onto the tatami. 'Itadakimasu!'

'Our teacher will be mad at us if we don't finish the visual aids today.'

'We'll be fine! But wow, yum! Eat already, Haruna!'

'Agh, if you rush like that, you'll get it on your shirt!'

Ryoko smiled watching them.

When Ryoko whispered, 'You two seem to get along awfully well,' in Haruna's ear, the girl blushed.

'Huh? No, it's not like that . . .'

'Oh? Are you sure?'

As the three of them were carrying on, Ken popped up. 'How far did you get?'

'We decided on a direction,' Eita said with his mouth full and then wiped it with a paper napkin before continuing. 'We decided we'll use one of the three posters to draw the display we designed. On the other two, we'll write about why we chose the theme of products that are easy to use for everyone and then the things we realised through our job shadowing or, like, what changed between before and after.'

'That sounds great. Oh, if you'll allow me to offer some friendly advice, I think you should write a script first. And then I think it would be good to do a rough draft on a newspaper instead of writing directly on the butcher paper. You almost never write on paper this big, right? It's hard to get a feel for how big the characters should be.' Ken advised them in a calm tone.

Haruna replied, 'Thank you. That's really helpful. But also . . . you know you have to write one, too, right?'

'What?!'

Haruna, Eita and Ryoko burst out laughing at how panicked he was.

'There's a section called "From the on-the-job manager" that you have to write. You should have got an email from our teacher . . .?'

Ken shook his head. 'I had no idea . . . What should I do, Ryoko?'

Ryoko laughed again at how lost he looked. 'Don't make such a pathetic face. I'll watch the shop today. Do your best!'

As the busy month of December approached, Ginza was getting colder with each passing day, but Shihodo's atmosphere was animated as usual.

Business Cards

'I'm heading out.' I stood as I heard the announcement over the PA signalling the end of the workday.

'See you . . .' A scattering of voices from the seats around me called. It was no different from any other day.

I glanced towards the section chief and department head's chairs, but they must have both been in a meeting. Not that anything would have been different if they had been at their desks.

At the end of the previous month, I had met with the section chief to discuss my leaving the company.

'Togawa-san, are you sure you want your last day at the office to be the day you retire? Seems like a waste. You have so much paid holiday left. Anyone else would let that run out and be done about two months early. Though I suppose every day's a holiday starting the next day, so it's not so different. Anyway, I'm jealous. I still have to work another twenty years.'

The section chief, who had turned forty the previous year, didn't look at me, but kept his eyes on his tablet. Maybe he was looking at the manual.

'Uh, next I need to collect your business cards.'

The cards had hardly been used since I'd made them, and I handed them over in the box.

'It's just a formality, since there could be trouble if someone misused them.'

Notes from the Ginza Shihodo Stationery Shop

What do they do about people who don't return a full box? I wondered, but didn't say anything. Besides, who would misuse the cards of a rank-and-file employee with no title?

'By the way, I need to ask what you'd like to do about a farewell party, parting words on your final day and so on . . .' the section chief continued as he opened the box and confirmed the contents.

'Ah, that's OK. I don't need any fanfare . . .'

'Oh, are you sure? Understood. Then we'll go with none. Well, our section is mainly temps and staff on loan from group companies anyway. OK, I'll report that to the department head,' the section chief announced unilaterally before hurrying out of the meeting room. I'm sure he was inwardly relieved. If there were going to be a party, he'd have to order someone to organise it, and if I were going to say a parting word on my last day, he would have had to prepare a bouquet. The only thing I could do for them now was limit the annoyances on my way out by practically disappearing.

When I got back to my seat, the section chief was handing my cards to another employee and saying, 'Shred these.' *He didn't have to do that where I could hear . . .* I thought.

I went down the stairs to the ground floor and walked quickly out of the entrance. At this time of day, there aren't very many employees hurrying home, so normally the 'See you tomorrow' of the security staffer would echo out. But today I didn't hear that voice. When I turned to look, I saw a young man who must have been a part-timer standing there absent-mindedly, awkward in his uniform.

'Err, is Yamamoto-san not here today?'

Business Cards

I thought I had seen him that morning.

'Ahh . . . He left around three saying he had an errand to run.'

'I see . . . Sorry to bother you. I'm heading out for the day.'

'No trouble at all. Good night.'

I replied to his clumsy bow by lowering my head before exiting through the automatic doors and going past the driveway to the street. I had decided not to turn around as I walked to the station, but before I realised, I had stopped to look up at the office building.

The view was completely different from forty years before. The old office building had been torn down years ago and a new, bigger one built in its place during a wave of redevelopment. Still, I felt there had to be something more to the building in front of me than mere inorganic architecture. I set my bag down, stood tall and bowed deeply.

At that moment, a powerful wind blew, loudly rustling the branches of the willow trees. Suddenly, the corners of my eyes felt hot, and I hurriedly straightened up. When I looked to the sky, I suppose because the season was such that there was still a chill in the air, it was completely dark, and a cloud was partially covering the brightly shining moon. Before I knew it, I was humming 'Ue o muite aruko' – even though I hated karaoke and had never sung the song before. *Yes, I'll look up as I head home, taking my usual route.*

When I turned the corner to head to the station, the familiar postbox was waiting for me. I took a postcard out of my coat pocket and slipped it into the old-fashioned, cylindrical box. With its big round face and gaping mouth, it seemed like a hungry glutton that might devour my hand along with the card.

Notes from the Ginza Shihodo Stationery Shop

Having turned in my computer and smartphone in the morning, I'd had nothing to do in the afternoon, so I'd written to my wife on a postcard I'd discovered in the back of a desk drawer.

Today, I'm officially retired. I wouldn't have been able to work this long without you. Thank you. Really, it'd be better if I could look you in the eye and say it, but I'd be embarrassed, so I'm writing it on a postcard. I hope you'll continue to support me.

The picture on the postcard was of the father and son lions from the dance *Renjishi* whipping their manes around; I couldn't for the life of me remember when I'd bought it. I used it since I didn't want to waste it, but I regretted not buying one with some flowers or a night view of Ginza. Still, I expected my wife would laugh and say it was very me.

I turned back around to my right to look at the postbox again. Behind it stood the venerable old stationery shop, Shihodo.

No matter when I looked, its appearance gave off an air of elegance, and the atmosphere Ginza had in the days I first came to Tokyo remained there vividly. I gazed at the shop absent-mindedly as I stood in the breeze.

When I first came to Tokyo, there were still many old buildings like Shihodo. Of course, areas that had been damaged due to the war, as well as the areas redeveloped for the Tokyo Olympics, were exceptions, but in Ginza, Yurakucho, Hibiya – that area – pre-war buildings remained.

They had been built during the Taisho or Showa eras,

Business Cards

yet they didn't feel old-fashioned; they appeared dignified and tasteful. The office of the company I joined was a building like that.

It was seven storeys in an art deco style and somehow reminiscent of the Whitehaven Mansions where the great detective Poirot was said to live. I remember well looking up at that beautiful building and thinking, *Yep, I got a job at a company in Tokyo – no, Ginza.*

I joined a food wholesaler listed in the first section of the Tokyo Stock Exchange, and at the time, the men they were hiring were almost all college graduates already. Nowadays, gender-based recruitment would be unthinkable, but back then it was normal. That's how it was, so I was the only man in my cohort with merely a high school diploma. Later, I heard that the guidance counsellor at my school and the HR manager were old friends, and it was due to their friendship that he bent over backwards to practically force me through.

In high school, the only class I took seriously was bookkeeping, and I'd got the level 2 certification, so I'd assumed I'd be put in Accounting, but the appointment I received was in General Affairs. Incidentally, all the guys with university education got assigned to Sales.

After the ceremony to welcome us and a picture taken for posterity, the university grads were put on a bus and taken to a training facility in the suburbs. They would live there for a month doing new employee training.

I found myself alone, but someone from HR took me over to my new team's office.

General Affairs was in a small room at the back of the building, next to the employee entrance. When I opened the door, no one was inside. There were four desks, some steel lockers, bookshelves and whatnot.

'This is the General Affairs office.' The HR person flicked the lights on. 'They told me your desk is here. You probably don't have much stuff, but if you want to leave some writing utensils, notebooks or what have you, you can use the drawer. Do you think you can get filled in on the rest tomorrow from the people in this department?'

'Sure ... Um, where are the other General Affairs employees?'

The HR fellow glanced at his watch and said, 'Well, they're probably not around at this time of day . . .' he grumbled. 'Togawa-kun, you can head home for today.'

'What? I feel like I should at least say hello to the department head ...'

'Well, yeah, but I don't think you'll be able to see him today.'

'Then the section chief? I should meet *someone* from General Affairs.'

He shook his head. 'You're the only one.'

'Huh?'

With an awkward expression, he murmured, 'Wow, they didn't explain anything . . .' and looked at me with pity in his eyes. 'Anyway, for today, you can go home. Oh, but, of course, you can put the regular ending time on your timecard. And then tomorrow, it's not to make up for leaving early, but you should get here by seven a.m.'

'Seven a.m.?' I'd heard the day started at nine.

'Yeah, that's what they told me to tell you. Actually, you should be ready to move at seven, so you might want to be here a little earlier than that. After all, you're a new employee.'

'I ... see ...'

Business Cards

'Yep. So you can head out once you put your stuff in your desk. Why not enjoy a stroll around Ginza? Well, that's it from me.'

With that, the HR guy left. Something didn't feel quite right, but I couldn't do anything about it, so I left early, as instructed, and went home. I was in no mood to stroll around Ginza by myself.

The next morning, I opened the door to General Affairs at six-thirty An older man was sitting there in workwear reading the news-paper, with a teacup in one hand. To be fair, he seemed to have a lot of vigour for an older guy.

'... U-umm.'

When I spoke up, he glared at me. 'Don't you mean, "Good morning"?'

When I hurriedly corrected to 'Good morning', he heaved a sigh and said, 'That was awfully quiet. Did you eat breakfast?'

'Huh? Err, yes.'

I'd eaten a simple breakfast of anpan and milk that I'd bought yesterday.

'Then make sure to greet people loudly. A new employee's most important job is to return greetings with plenty of energy. If you can do that, you pass. Though it's not as easy as it seems.'

'Oh . . .'

'Right, so not, "Oh . . ." but, "I see!"'

'I see.'

'No, not like that . . . OK, you gotta get in the habit of focusing on each separate syllable and saying them clearly! Like, if it were written out, we want angular *katakana* not soft, round *hiragana*! Enunciate!'

'"I see"?'

The old man burst out laughing. 'You really . . . Well, it's fine. More importantly, you're awfully relaxed. What time do you think it is?'

I checked my watch in a panic.

'Err, I was told to be here by seven.'

'If you're told to be somewhere by seven, you can't go arriving at seven. If you're told seven, you need to be there by six. If you're told six, then it's five.'

Nowadays, this would probably count as power harassment. Or maybe moral harassment? But back then those concepts didn't even exist. And, strangely, I didn't question what I was being told. The thought simply came to mind that adults have it rough.

'. . . OK, I understand.'

But the old man heaved a sigh and shook his head.

'I can tell you're not convinced. Look, you won't be able to do a decent job unless you change your way of thinking. You need to be terribly, terribly concerned about arriving on time no matter what. And lots of things will happen! But no matter what happens, it's an excuse. That's how bad it is to not show up at the time you agreed on. Remember that!' Then he said, 'All right, shall we get started?' and stood up. 'For starters, get changed.'

'Get changed?'

Without answering, he opened one of the steel lockers. Inside hung a grey outfit like the one he was wearing. There was also a pair of black rubber boots.

'I'm sure your parents shelled out for those fancy clothes, so it would be a shame to get them dirty. Change into this. Shoes included.'

Business Cards

Unable to grasp this development, I stood there in a daze. The old man said, 'Come out the side door when you're ready,' and left the room.

Since I had no other choice, I changed into the work clothes and boots. They were all new and needed to be broken in, but they fit perfectly.

When I poked my head out of the door, I found the old man waiting with a broom, dustpan, bin bags and other cleaning supplies.

'We'll start with sweeping. You go from that corner towards the office; I'll come from the opposite direction.'

The corner he pointed to was easily a hundred metres away.

'From that far . . .?'

'Who cleans only their own area? If you appreciate your neighbours and want to give back a little, tidying up is the least you can do. Now, get going. Oh, take a bin bag. If you don't dump the dustpan often, the wind will scatter everything.'

After handing me a bag, he turned and walked off. With no other option, I walked in the opposite direction. Pacing away with our backs to each other felt like the showdown scene in a Western, but instead of a pistol, I was carrying a broom and dustpan.

Nowadays, far fewer people smoke, so you don't often see cigarette butts littering the street, but back then there were quite a lot. And worse, sometimes – maybe the person was in a foul mood – the butts were ground into dust, which made them hard to sweep up. There was all sorts of other stuff lying around, too: tissues, flyers from bars and restaurants, evening newspapers, magazines . . .

The road in front of the office was barely wide enough for

two cars to pass each other, but sweeping it properly end to end still took a while. After I'd done about half, I turned around to find the old man standing nearby.

'You're not done yet?'

The opposite area he said he would handle was already neat and clean.

'. . . Sorry.'

'Well, you're not used to it, so it can't be helped. But it's taking you too long because you're not using the broom right. Watch closely.'

He used the tip of the broom to flip the cigarette butt I'd been battling with into the dustpan in no time.

'Use the tip to flick the rubbish together. Where it's tricky to sweep flat, stand it more upright. When you want to pull something out of a tight spot, use the broom's corner like this. A little ingenuity goes a long way. Well, once you get the hang of it, it'll go faster.'

As the old man helped me sweep, I started to notice company employees showing up early among the passers-by on the street. Whenever someone approached, the old man always paused to say, 'Good morning!' with a lowered head.

'What are you standing around for? You say it too.'

'Huh? Oh. G-good morning . . .'

I hurriedly bowed, but everyone just passed by with barely a bob of their heads.

'Oh my word, why is your voice so pitiful? Did you really eat breakfast? You need to say, "Good morning!" clearly, with more pep! They can't hear you!'

'Mm . . . Do you know that person?'

'I don't know his name. But he walks past here every morning.

He wears a suit, so he must work for one of the companies around here. Oh, good morning!'

The old man paused again to greet someone. I echoed him in a hurry.

'Well, that's a bit of an improvement. But I'm sure you can project better than that, can't you? Greeting people in a loud voice feels good. And the person you're talking to won't feel bad about it, either. They may only bob their heads in reply, but in their hearts, I'm sure they've accepted your greeting.'

I don't think I've been advised so sternly about greetings since I was an elementary schooler.

As we were cleaning and greeting, someone I'd seen sitting on the raised platform at the ceremony to welcome new recruits – probably an executive – arrived. I was shocked to see him stride over to the old man and bow deeply to say, 'Good morning, Chairman, I see you're working hard as usual.'

'Chairman?!' I yelped without thinking.

'What, you didn't know?' the old man smiled.

One executive had been absent from the ceremony. The seat was labelled Chairman and Executive Director. I thought maybe he would be late, but in the end, he never showed up. That guy was now dressed in workwear, zealously sweeping the street.

After eight, the number of employees showing up jumped, and everyone said, 'Good morning, Chairman!' as they passed. And every time, the chairman said, 'Ohhh, morning!' or 'You sound great. How's it going?' or 'I heard you were in the hospital. All better now?' replying to each and every one of them. He looked genuinely happy to see them. His expression was like a grandfather interacting with a cute kid or grandchild.

When we were done sweeping, we mopped the tiles at the

Notes from the Ginza Shihodo Stationery Shop

front entrance and polished the glass doors. After cleaning, putting away the supplies and washing our hands, the nine o'clock chime rang to announce the start of the workday.

'Well, it's actually time to start work, but let's take a break first. Today we got off to a late start. Tomorrow let's try to up the pace a bit and be done by 8:30,' said the chairman as he made me some tea. My hands had got cold washing the rags and mop, so the warm cup felt nice to hold.

'Umm . . . yesterday I heard from HR that I'm the only person in the General Affairs department. Is it just General Affairs in name while the job is cleaning?'

'Naw. The head of HR is also the head of General Affairs. But that's in name only – the work is handled by a pair of non-regular employees. They're former employees who both retired years ago. In exchange for a low salary, they're allowed to come and go pretty freely. I mean, I think they'll show up soon, but . . .'

Just as he finished explaining, the door to General Affairs opened.

'Huh? Do you have time to be puttering around down here, sir?'

'Yeah, isn't the board meeting today? If you don't hurry upstairs, your secretaries will be losing their minds.'

'See? I told you,' he said when I was speechless. 'It's because you two weren't here yet. I was waiting for you! This is the new recruit I told you about.'

'I'm Togawa, Iwao Togawa.' I rushed to my feet and bowed.

'Iwao, this old fellow is Maruta-san and this old lady is Kakuta-san. Here everyone knows them as Maru-san and Kaku-chan from General Affairs. They know everything there is to know about the company, so learn well. Take good care of him, you two! Show him the ropes and turn him into a General Affairs guy we can trust to handle anything. Don't go kicking the bucket until you've trained him up!'

'If we kick the bucket, the cause of death will be you working us too hard, sir!' Kaku-chan laughed.

'Yeah, and more importantly, you really shouldn't overdo it, sir. You call us old, but you're a good bit older.' Maru-san cracked a smile, but his brow was furrowed.

'Yeah, I'm aware. Well, I guess I should head upstairs.'

He clapped me on the shoulder and left the room.

'Togawa-sama.'

I was surprised to suddenly hear my name. At some point, someone had appeared at the stationery shop's entrance.

'Oh, Takarada-san, hello. Or I suppose it's "Good evening" at this point.'

The company used to get all our writing materials, business cards and so on from Shihodo, but some years ago we switched to ordering online. I still stopped by occasionally to pick up the organiser or stationery I was accustomed to. Though that will end today. I don't expect I'll be coming to Ginza very often anymore.

Takarada-san was dressed in his usual light blue shirt, navy tie, grey trousers and black leather shoes. He's young, in his late thirties, but when you consult with him on something, no matter how small, he handles it with care.

He came out to the postbox, bobbed his head, and continued, 'I thought you might be passing by soon, so I was keeping an eye out. Ah, I'm glad you didn't take some other route home today . . . So, your many years of work have come to an end.'

This surprised me again. I had the feeling I'd mentioned

maybe six months ago, 'The next time the plums blossom, I'll be retirement age,' but I didn't recall saying anything about when exactly I would retire.

'Oh, yes, it's today. I didn't realise you knew.'

'Of course I do! After all, you're a very important long-time patron of the shop.'

Even in the knowledge that it was flattery, I didn't feel bad.

'I don't think I bought enough to be called a patron.'

'Don't be silly. Would you like to stop by for a moment?'

'Hmm, I suppose I could . . .'

Where does a normal person stop by on their retirement day? I suddenly wondered. Do they part the rope curtain at their favourite *izakaya* and have a quiet beer by themselves? Or maybe they go to a cafe where they used to eat lunch and leisurely give themselves over to the scent of the coffee? But I didn't have any places like that. If I was a regular anywhere, it was Shihodo.

'Sure, for a little while.'

'Great, thank you.'

Takarada-san carried himself gracefully as he led me to the glass door, which he opened for me like the doorman of a hotel.

Inside, there was no music, just a faint aroma in the air. He must have been burning incense, but I didn't see it anywhere, and I wasn't sure what the scent was. I felt as if I had stepped into another world.

'This place never changes, huh?' I murmured without really meaning to.

Takarada-san scratched the back of his head self-consciously. 'I mean, I do refresh the special displays regularly and try to add some accents here and there . . .' I couldn't help but laugh at how ashamed he seemed.

Business Cards

'Sorry, sorry – I didn't mean it in a bad way! I'm happy that no matter when I come, this place is the Shihodo I love.'

Takarada-san smiled with relief for a moment before immediately zipping his lips back together and continuing. 'If you say so . . . A friend of mine from middle school runs a *wagashi* shop near here. He's found great success by sticking to the venerable shop's traditional methods while at the same time boldly creating – I suppose you could say, innovative? – new sweets. It feels like the kid I used to kick a football around with has moved far beyond me . . . So that's been making me wonder recently if I can really just continue on with this straight-ahead, honest-to-a-fault business style . . .'

Takarada-san's eyes seemed to waver.

'What are you talking about? What's so bad about honesty? I don't think there's a thing wrong with it. On the contrary, I hope you'll stay honest to a fault.' Even I was surprised by how forceful my tone was. '. . . Sorry, maybe I raised my voice too much,' I said, bowing my head, and Takarada-san got flustered.

'None of that! It can't be good luck for me to make a customer feel like that! Besides . . . it's out of character for me to be so vulnerable and I shouldn't have burdened you. Especially since it's an important day for you! I'm the one who should be apologising.'

He bowed, and it was my turn to be flustered. We shared a smile and proceeded to the back of the shop. When I looked out the window, the wind must have picked up, because I saw the branches of the willow trees swaying hard.

'Something I've been wondering for a while is . . . how come willow trees these days stay green even in winter?' I abruptly said what came to mind.

Notes from the Ginza Shihodo Stationery Shop

'Oh yeah?'

'Yes, isn't it strange? Willows are deciduous, so they should change colour in the autumn and then lose their leaves in the winter, but these days the willows in Ginza are green all year round. It's like they've stopped ageing...'

Takarada-san glanced at my face before returning his gaze to the road.

'This is second-hand knowledge from a customer, but... First, the willows on the streets of Ginza are *Salix babylonica*. These get pruned over the summer. Pruning them stimulates new growth, so autumn comes before the new leaves are mature. That's why they don't change colour or shed leaves even in the cold.'

'Ohhh.'

Takarada-san nodded emphatically to my vacant reply.

'At any rate, it's important to keep the willows looking nice for the landscape, but I also appreciate that I don't have to sweep up a ton of fallen leaves.'

'I bet. That's a lot of work. For a month or so, no matter how much you sweep, there seem to always be more leaves. It's especially hard after it rains and they're plastered to the ground.'

'True... Togawa-sama, you worked in General Affairs, right? Were you also in charge of cleaning?'

I looked at his face for just a moment, but immediately returned my gaze to the road.

'No, by the time I joined the company they had already outsourced the cleaning of the office, but the exterior wasn't part of the contract. Well, it was like training. Cleaning the street wasn't a job anyone wanted, and no one would praise you for doing it.'

I fixed my eyes on the willow branches whipping in the wind.

*

Business Cards

My mornings cleaning with the chairman continued. In those days, we worked on Saturday as well, and with Sundays, holidays, three days for Obon, and four days for the New Year, even all together it was only slightly over sixty days off. Nowadays, we have over double the holiday, and I appreciate how much it has grown.

The routine was to clean every workday, and I showed up at the office at 6 a.m. I gradually got used to waking up early, and by autumn, it was no longer a pain for me to get to work by six. One Monday, I decided to ask the chairman about something I happened to notice.

'Considering we didn't clean yesterday because it was Sunday, there's not much rubbish around. Is it just because there aren't very many people around on Sunday?'

The chairman gave me an incredulous look. 'What are you talking about? Ginza is packed on Sundays and holidays. People come from all over the place to shop, eat out . . .'

'Ohhh, I didn't know.'

'Not that that's the reason or anything, but I clean on our days off too. I want to make sure Ginza looks nice for the people coming from out of town!'

'What? You clean on our days off?'

The chairman made a face that said, *Shoot!* and clicked his tongue. 'Listen, don't misunderstand. I'm not telling you to come and clean on your days off. I live in the neighbourhood and walk past here every day. So I just tidy up a little bit when I happen to pass by, that's all. So don't go getting weirdly considerate or anything.'

'. . . OK.'

I was a bit surprised.

Notes from the Ginza Shihodo Stationery Shop

'Also, Ginza on a day off is different from a workday. It has its own charms.'

'What's so great about it?'

'I wonder how to put it . . . I'm not sure I can explain well. Right . . . it's like the whole town is excited, and it smells nice somehow. There's this fun – or, like, joyful? – kind of atmosphere.'

What kind of atmosphere might that be? I tried to picture it.

'Are you telling me you've never come out?'

'I haven't. My day off is over by the time I'm done with cleaning and laundry. I sleep in till around noon, to begin with . . . And I've only ever walked the road from the station to the office, so I hardly even know workday Ginza . . .'

The chairman shook his head with a genuinely frustrated look on his face. 'That's such a waste when the company pays for your monthly train pass to Ginza. Plus, if you work in Ginza, don't you tell your girlfriend you'll bring her to a restaurant you know sometime?'

'. . . I've never been out with a woman.'

'Nnngh, then don't you go and see a film with friends? Or grab a cup of coffee at a cafe? There must be something.'

I hung my head and poked the ground with my broom. 'I'm the only high school grad in my cohort. They're all four years older than me, so they don't even treat me as part of the group. Plus, the friends I came to Tokyo with all work for factories in Fuchu or Kawasaki. It's not so easy to go and see them. And the train fare would be crazy expensive.'

Hearing my response, the chairman fell silent. He seemed to be thinking. 'I see . . .'

His voice was so down, I rushed to say, 'Oh, but there is a

Business Cards

library near my room. I borrow books, so it's not as if I'm bored. It's free, and I can learn things . . .'

The chairman shook his head slightly. 'It's great to be into studying, but what's important for you right now isn't cramming your head full of new information, it's having new experiences. In other words, try deviating from your usual route once in a while. I'm sure you'll find a world you've never known. It could even change your whole life.'

'Oh . . .'

'I think you meant, "I see!"' he corrected. 'All right! I have an administrative order for you!'

'Huh? Wh-what is it?'

I'd never received an administrative order from Maru-san or Kaku-chan. At most, it would be errands like, 'Please deliver these papers to Accounting,' 'Be a dear and line up the tables and chairs in the meeting room and set out the ashtrays,' 'Could you buy some pens and carbon paper?'

'Oh, it's nothing to worry about! Just, starting today, I want you to go home using a different route to the station each day for a while.'

'Every day?'

My dubious expression must have been awfully funny, because the chairman burst out laughing.

'That's right. Really I'd like to tell you to come in by a different route, too, but it'd be a problem for me if you got lost on your way and were late to cleaning.'

Actually, I have a terrible sense of direction, to the point that even just to run an errand in the neighbourhood of the office, I slipped a map into my chest pocket.

'Report to me the next day while we're cleaning about what

route you took, what you saw. If you find an interesting-looking place, stop in! Hmm . . .' The chairman pulled out his wallet, casually pulled out some notes and stuffed them in my breast pocket. 'That's funding for this project. Don't you dare go saving it! Spend it like you're supposed to. You can go and see some kabuki or eat something you think looks tasty. You could even go to a bar or cabaret. Oh wait, you're underage so you can't drink.'

I pulled the cash out of my pocket in a panic. They were all 10,000-yen notes — there had to be at least 300,000 yen.

'I-I can't accept all this.'

'It's not a loan — it's an investment.'

'But . . . there's no way I'll be able to spend this much money . . .'

The chairman's jaw dropped. 'Listen, one night at a high-class club and it's gone. Well, if you don't have enough, just give them my business card and tell them to bill me. That should work at most places in Ginza. I'll have my secretary give you some cards.'

After this, every day was a little bit of an adventure for me.

That said, the things a kid who arrived from the country six months ago could do were fairly limited. On the first day, I stopped at a venerable old bookshop on Ginza Dori and bought a guide to Ginza in which I found a cafe attached to a fruit shop where I ate a fruit parfait. Besides domestically grown, high-quality melon and peaches, there were generous helpings of imported tropical fruits such as pineapple, papaya and mango, plus accents of ice cream and whipped cream — the parfait was so delicious, it seemed like something from another world.

The next day when I reported to the chairman, his face crinkled into a smile and he simply said, 'Good for you!'

'Err, I brought a receipt . . .'

Business Cards

When I said that, the chairman put his hand out. I rushed to hand over the receipt I'd had prepared, but he threw it into a bin bag without even looking at it.

'That's my money, so though I told you it's an administrative order, it has nothing to do with the company. So there's no need to bring receipts. Well, maybe it's good to have them as you learn what things cost, so I won't tell you not to get them, but you never have to show me. Like I said yesterday, I'm investing in you. As long as you use it for your personal growth, that's fine...'

'Yes, sir...' I knew I'd be scolded if I didn't reply loudly, but the backs of my eyes felt hot, and my voice wouldn't come out.

'Oh, but don't tell anyone, OK? This is our secret.'

From then on, in order to even slightly meet his expectations, I pored over the guidebook and went to all sorts of places. This was when I learned how interesting kabuki is. I also developed my palate at famous sushi restaurants and places serving other kinds of cuisine, as well as specialty coffee and tea shops.

It always seemed to be the days that I was about to report what tasty thing I'd eaten that we'd find vomit splattered on the road. The chairman would always say, 'I'll handle this,' and never made me do it.

'But... I'll do it.'

'No, if I ever want to leave this sort of unpleasant work to others, I'll retire.'

He was stubborn. But then, when I didn't leave, he'd say, 'Well, fine. I'm sure you'll climb the ranks someday, so in order for you to be able to teach others how to do it, go ahead and watch. Times like this, don't be so lazy that you don't wear disposable gloves and a mask. Probably it's just someone who threw up because he drank too much, but it could also be a present from someone who got bested by a nasty illness. Not to brag, but I failed in that way once, too. Three whole days I was so nauseous I couldn't drink any water and had non-stop diarrhoea. Thanks to that I lost five kilos!'

Grinning as he put on his gloves and mask, he first covered the mess with newspaper. Then, folding the paper from the edges towards the middle, he wiped up the filth and threw it into the bin bag. Surprisingly, he managed to get it so clean that only a faint stain remained on the tarmac.

Then he used a ratty old rag that seemed about ready to be trashed and scrubbed at the stain and washed everything into the gutter with a bucket of water.

'There! Clean, right?' When he took his mask off, his upper lip was soaked with sweat.

'Yes, excellent work. But I can't help but think it's not a job for you, sir. Really, it should be the person who had the accident who should clean it up. If you're going to throw up like that, you shouldn't be drinking.'

Even I found it unusual how upset I was about this.

'Well, you're right, of course, but there are some times you can't make it without drinking, sometimes in life you gotta drink even though you know you'll throw up. You'll learn soon enough.'

'Is that true . . .?'

The chairman nodded deeply and looked up at the blue sky. 'I wonder how the fellow who threw up here is doing now. I hope that since he vomited up everything in his stomach, he's at work doing well as if nothing happened.'

I looked at his face in profile and thought, *This is the man whose footsteps I want to follow in.*

*

Business Cards

'Thanks. I really do love Shihodo.' After taking a look around the shop, I turned to Takarada-san. 'Since I retired from the company, I probably won't come out to Ginza much, but if I do, I'll be sure to stop by.'

'I see . . . Oh, Togawa-sama, you've never been upstairs, have you?' He glanced towards the staircase at the back of the shop.

'Nope, I haven't. Though I know you rent the space out for seal-carving and printmaking workshops. I'm clumsy so I never felt like giving any of it a try.'

'Would you like to take a look? There's also a landing partway up that gives you an overhead view of the shop.'

That did sound worthwhile. I'd actually seen someone looking out over the ground floor from the landing before.

'Right this way.'

Seeing the courteous way he ushered me towards the stairs, I realised something. I'd thought for a while that Takarada-san resembled someone, and now I knew who: the manager of a restaurant that had closed quite some time ago.

As if in proportion to my efforts at coming up with new ways home on the chairman's order, I was gradually given different kinds of General Affairs tasks. Physical labour, especially, was impossible for Maru-san and Kaku-chan to handle, so that all fell to me. As a result, despite being a new employee, I was able to visit every department and get a lot of more experienced co-workers to recognise me.

Once they knew me, they started to ask me to help out with things that weren't actually General Affairs tasks. At first, it was small things: 'Can I borrow you for just thirty minutes?' or 'I really need to get this done fast . . .' but as we headed into winter, there were more and more requests.

'Togawa-kun, sorry, but could I ask you to prep some materials for tomorrow's meeting?'

'It's about the new catalogue. I need to mail out quite a few copies. We're in a pinch, so could you help out this afternoon?'

The amount of overtime I was doing rapidly increased, so I had less and less time to go on my after-work adventures.

'Sorry, yesterday I stayed late helping the Sales team . . .'

The chairman glanced at my face for a moment before shaking his head slightly. 'If people are relying on you, that means the number of people who see that you can handle work has increased. That's not a bad thing. But it's no reason to go straight home! Ginza is a town of night owls.'

'I thought you might say that. Last night, I noticed there were some stalls out behind the kabuki theatre. I had some oden, but it had some kind of western-style seasoning; it was tasty. I was surprised to find food stalls in Ginza.'

'There were more in the older days. Well, for now concentrate on the days you have time to take a detour. After all, it's a good thing that more people have recognised your abilities – for you and for me.'

It kind of seemed like he was praising me, which made me happy.

'Sir?'

'Hm? What is it?'

'I got my first bonus the other day. Thank you.'

At the time, it was customary for new employees to get their first bonus in the winter.

'Hmm, thanking me is a misunderstanding. The company

Business Cards

paid you that in acknowledgement of the work you've been doing. You can accept it with confidence. Though it's true that me and the other executives decide the amounts . . . We were only able to give you a little bit. Sorry, but please make do.' He straightened up and bowed.

'Oh, no, it's great! I'm only about as useful as a maid, so I didn't even expect to get a bonus.'

That was how I really felt.

'Oh? If you say so . . .'

I knew that all the other guys who joined the company at the same time as me had better salaries, too.

'There is one favour I wanted to ask, though . . .'

'Huh? A request from you is awfully rare.'

'I was wondering if you would come with me on a detour some night when you're free.'

He frowned. 'I guess I don't mind . . .'

'Thank you! And while I'm being selfish, could we invite Maru-san and Kaku-chan as well?'

'Hmm? I mean, sure . . .'

Strike while the iron is hot, as they say. I ended up getting some of the chairman's time a mere three days later.

'Then, we're off.'

I headed for a certain Ginza alley, leading the three who had gathered.

'It's been quite some time since I've strolled Ginza at night!' Kaku-chan smiled happily. She'd dressed up a little more than usual.

'Same . . .' Maru-san nodded, decked out in a suit.

'I haven't been out like this in a while either, except for dinners with clients.' The chairman nodded deeply, looking like a totally different person from when he was dressed in work clothes and boots. When you think about it, the chairman was a businessman who had built a little food-wholesaling business into a listed company in a single generation – not really the sort of person I, basically an apprentice, should have been inviting out.

I was hit with a sudden wave of anxiety, but it was too late for regrets.

Before long, we arrived at the restaurant I'd been aiming for. When we opened the door to find the host standing by, and when I said I had a reservation, we were shown to a table for four.

'Oh-ho, so this is your favourite place, huh, Iwao?' the chairman murmured once we had taken our seats, as if he understood completely.

'Is beer good for everyone? I've never ordered alcohol before, so I have no idea . . .'

The three of them nodded.

'It's good manners for guests to accept whatever their host has prepared, so whatever you've thought up for us is great, Iwao.'

The chairman's comment was a relief. I'd been wondering what I would do if they wanted to drink wine. It was way too complicated for me – I never would've been able to handle it.

The manager who had taken my reservation noticed us and approached.

'We'd like the order I put in originally.'

The manager nodded with a soft, 'Of course,' and bowed deeply before returning to the kitchen.

A big, well-chilled bottle of beer and three glasses were produced immediately, as well as water for me. With shaking hands, I poured everyone's beer.

Business Cards

Then, with their full glasses in hand, they all turned their gazes on me.

'Don't just stare! Say a word before we drink!'

Kaku-chan's nudge made me panic. 'What?! Me?'

'Of course, you. You're the one who invited us, Togawa-chan!' Maru-san rolled his eyes, while the chairman just nodded.

'What? Uhhh . . . Then . . . thank you for taking time out of your busy schedules to join me tonight. And . . . I appreciate all your help over the past eight months since April. I'm a slow learner, but you taught me patiently, never giving up, and I was even able to receive a bonus. While it could never express my full gratitude, I decided to plan this dinner. I hope you'll all have a relaxing evening.'

The chairman clapped softly. Kaku-chan and Maru-san followed his lead by nodding.

'Cheers, everyone!'

'Cheers!'

It was a very quiet cheers. After I filled their empty glasses, the chairman took the bottle from me and said, 'From now on we'll just all go at our own pace. You can relax, too, Iwao.' And then he complimented me. 'That was a great speech. What was so good about it was that you were able to speak in your own words. Your emotions came through clearly. You don't need to be all stiff and formal. As long as you make sure each word comes from the heart, your meaning will be understood.'

'. . . I see.'

It was the first time he had praised me so thoroughly, and I was really happy.

'And best of all, it was short!' said Maru-san, draining the rest of his beer.

'It's true. The execs all go on for sooo long. Don't they know that a greeting like that is better the shorter it is?' Kaku-chan said, nodding deeply.

'I'm a bit of an exec myself, you know,' grumbled the chairman.

'Oh, sorry! I forgot!'

Everyone laughed.

The menu I'd ordered arrived dish by dish: salad garnished with smoked salmon, consommé and grilled chicken as the main. Everyone was smiling, and I was so happy. I remember thinking, *So this is what it means to entertain company.*

'Apologies for the wait. Your *omuraisu*.'

The omelette rice I'd ordered to round out the meal was served. When I glanced at the clock, I saw it had already been an hour and a half since we'd arrived.

After setting out each dish, the waiter topped them all with bright red tomato sauce.

'Wow, the yellow of the eggs really makes the red of the sauce pop! It looks delicious.' Kaku-chan beamed. It was such a youthful smile – more like a young girl's – that you'd never have guessed she'd passed her sixtieth birthday years ago.

'Omuraisu, huh? I haven't had this in ages. Looks tasty!' Maru-san chimed in as he adjusted the position of the napkin in his lap. Next to him, the chairman already had his spoon in his mouth.

'Mm-hmm, mm-hmm. Yum, yum.'

'Phew . . .' I'd murmured in relief before I realised. 'When I first came here, I couldn't believe how good the omuraisu was. Like – could something so delicious actually exist in this world?'

'Wow, and instead of keeping it to yourself, you decided

Business Cards

to share it with all of us. That's what makes you such a good guy, Togawa-chan.' Maru-san smiled as he lifted his spoon to his lips.

'. . . I appreciate it.' The chairman's voice was filled with emotion.

'Oh, but . . . this is nothing compared to everything you've done for me. Maru-san, Kaku-chan, that goes the same for you.'

'. . . No. I, I . . . I haven't eaten a meal this good in a long time. Thank you – really, Iwao. Thank you for the lovely dinner.'

At the chairman's words, Maru-san and Kaku-chan both bowed their heads to me.

'Oh, but you don't need to . . . Agh . . . Well, let's order some after-dinner drinks. Coffee's good for everyone, right?'

I stood up in a hurry – because I felt if I stayed in my seat I would end up crying.

The manager, standing by in the corner of the room, noticed me.

'Four coffees, please. Also, I'd like to take care of the bill ahead of time . . .'

The manager said, 'Very well,' and whispered something in our waiter's ear before saying, 'Right this way,' and inviting me to the reception desk.

'Thank you. With your help, I was able to entertain the people who have been taking care of me at work.'

Nodding at my comment, he glanced at the envelope I'd taken out of my pocket and said, 'One moment, please,' before disappearing into the back.

After a short wait, he returned with a man wearing a chef's hat.

'This is the owner.'

Notes from the Ginza Shihodo Stationery Shop

The man bowed his head deeply. I returned the gesture, flustered.

'Thank you for dining here today. I don't mean to pry, but what was the occasion?'

'I wanted to thank the people at my company who have been taking such good care of me . . . I received my first bonus the other day, so I thought I would use that . . . I wasn't sure where to take them but finally felt I wanted them to taste your omuraisu.'

I realised they were both eyeing the envelope clutched in my hands. At the time, bonuses were paid in cash, and I'd kept it untouched for this day.

'I see . . . It's an honour to be chosen for such an important moment. I hope you'll keep us in mind if there's ever another important occasion.'

The chef bowed once more before disappearing back into the kitchen.

'That must have felt sudden – my apologies. As for the bill, here you are.'

The slip he handed me was far less than what I'd expected.

'Um . . . I think you must have miscalculated.'

I held out the bill, flustered, but the manager shook his head.

'No, please pay the amount listed. You've rewarded us quite well already, Togawa-sama.'

'What?'

'We were able to witness you so thoughtfully entertain people you feel indebted to. We felt we caught a glimpse of the spirit of hospitality, our starting point, that we restauranteurs must never forget. Please do come again.' He gave me a deep bow.

Business Cards

On my way home, I was thinking it over, and I guess maybe they saw me about to pay from such a slim-looking envelope, and it made them feel something.

'What do you think? I feel a bit sheepish tooting my own horn, but I do think it's quite nice.'

On the landing Takarada-san guided me to were a small table and two chairs. He pulled one out for me – 'Have a seat' – so I sat down.

'I see . . .' I murmured before I realised. Past the handrail, I could see the sales floor below and the road out of the window with its waving willow leaves. Shifting my gaze to the entrance, I saw that the glass doors were almost like a frame for the postbox. 'Yes, this *is* nice.'

I leaned on the railing and looked down at the sales floor absent-mindedly.

'Thank you. We have one long-time regular who always looks forward to drinking a cup of takeout coffee here.'

'Ooh, I'm jealous . . .'

Takarada-san's courteous demeanour really did remind me of the manager at that restaurant.

'I'm pretty sure you did some major remodelling, so it's amazing that the atmosphere of the shop hasn't changed one bit.'

'Thank you. We ripped up the flooring and reused it after a good polish. And we did our best to recreate the walls using the same type of plaster as when the shop was originally built. I made things difficult for the artisans, so it did end up costing a fair amount . . .'

That was a bit unexpected.

'So is this the original floor?'

Notes from the Ginza Shihodo Stationery Shop

'Yes. The placing is a little different, but the materials are the ones it was originally built with.'

Then that means the chairman must have set foot on this floor as well ... I mused.

Before I knew it, I'd been working for nearly three years. At the end of March, the new fiscal year was about to start, and the new recruits were about to join. I arrived back at the General Affairs office after setting up for the welcome ceremony to find a note on my desk:

When you reach a good stopping point, drop by the chairman's office.

I could tell from the handwriting's quirks that it was from Kaku-chan. When I rushed to the chairman's room, I found him there waiting for me in a suit.

'You could dress a little sharper ... Well, no matter. It's just you and me, anyway ...'

I'd been doing all sorts of physical work – arranging desks and chairs into rows, hanging the celebratory red-and-white banner – so I'd taken my tie off and rolled up my sleeves.

'Oh, I'm sorry. I was prepping for the welcome ceremony ...'

He came out from behind his desk, straightened up and looked me square in the eye. Faced with a more serious expression than I'd ever seen on him before, I felt my back straighten on its own.

'I wanted to give this to you personally.'

He approached and handed me what he was holding. In a clear plastic case were business cards with my name on them.

'All the university grads you joined the company with are being promoted to supervisor. Unfortunately, the president and

Business Cards

other management created a bylaw that says we don't promote high school grads within the first five years. I told them not to go making unfair rules and resisted, but . . . the odds were against me. Instead, I forced them to let me at least give you these. Sorry it was all I could manage.'

The title on my brand-new business cards was printed in small type: DEPUTY SUPERVISOR.

'Oh, but . . . I'm so incapable. You didn't have to do that for me.'

I bowed my head. No one had ever made me business cards before. At the time, the rule was that unless you were in Sales, taking meetings outside the company, you couldn't make business cards until you were supervisor level or higher.

The chairman responded with a vigorous shake of his head. 'Incapable? Don't be ridiculous. Haven't you done the morning cleaning for three years straight without skipping any days – even in the rain, even when it's windy? During the typhoon, you stayed over at the office without sleeping, keeping watch; and if it snowed, you naturally shovelled the mountain of snow outside. Who else did that besides you? No one's capable of it! Plus, on top of working hard at your own job in General Affairs, you continue to help with the tasks of any department that needs it with no complaints. Really, the supervisor title is meant to go to those who work themselves to the bone for others.'

I never imagined he would say something like that, and my heart trembled violently.

'Thank you.' When I bowed low, tears dripped onto the carpet.

'Sorry, please make do for a little longer. I'll get them to remove the "deputy" as soon as I can.'

I accepted the cards from the chairman with both hands.

Notes from the Ginza Shihodo Stationery Shop

'Now then, this is a different topic entirely, but I have a favour to ask of you. I want you to hold onto this for me.'

He handed me a key.

'What's this the key to?'

'It opens the safe in the corner.'

He gestured with his chin to a large safe occupying the corner.

'I'm headed into the hospital, so I won't be here for a while. I want you to take care of this key for me while I'm gone.'

'What . . .?'

The chairman looked at me and said, 'Don't look so worried!' with a laugh. 'Doctors always make such a big deal out of everything. There's something bugging him, so he says he wants to do a thorough check – even though I know my body best and I told him nothing's wrong. Oh, are you more worried about the key than my health? Well, that's not a big deal, either. Almost everything has been moved into the bank's vault. But it does contain the company's seal and my seal as representative director. For that reason, you'll need to open it a few times a day.'

'Seals . . .?'

'Yes, but not just any seals. These are registered with the government. If they were misused, the company could go bankrupt. That's how important they are.' The chairman went back behind his desk, set the key on it and took out a piece of paper. 'To open the safe, this unlock request is required; the safe can't be opened unless it's stamped with the seals of the heads of General Affairs and Accounting. Your job is to check the form to make sure it has both seals and then open the safe. And if the form doesn't have both seals, don't open the safe under any circumstances. Got it?'

Business Cards

'Is it really OK for me of all people to handle such an important key?' I looked between the key and the form on the desk.

'What are you saying? Who else could I trust with something this important?' He plucked the key off the desk and offered it to me. I put the business cards in my pocket and reverently accepted the key with two hands. 'I'm counting on you, Deputy Supervisor Togawa.'

'... Yes, sir.'

The chairman broke into a smile. 'Put a little more pep into that reply! Were you too busy to eat lunch, or something?' Though he had to just be joking around, there were tears in his eyes.

'Yes, sir!' I meant to project from the pit of my stomach, but my voice cracked.

'What was that?!'

'I mean ...'

I couldn't say it. The chairman nodded a few times in silence.

'Anyhow, starting tomorrow, I won't be around to clean for a while. You'll be on your own, but can you keep it up?'

'Yes, sir!'

That was how the chairman entrusted me with both the key and the road-cleaning.

On a Saturday about two months after I'd been given the key, I was getting ready to leave after finishing up some overtime when the head of Corporate Planning came to General Affairs.

'Hey, Togawa, bust out the key to the safe.'

I looked up at the clock and saw it was past seven.

'Sure, right away. Oh, but may I first see your unlock request?'

I stood up and hurried towards the door.

'Unlock request? Ah, I'll do the formalities later. This contract needs to be stamped, pronto. I'll get the paperwork in order later, so please just open the safe.'

The head of Corporate Planning was the chairman's son, and he had a reputation for being pushy.

'But rules are rules . . . The chairman told me in no uncertain terms that I was not to open the safe unless the unlock request had the seals of both the head of General Affairs and the head of Accounting.'

The head of Corporate Planning snorted. 'Uh-huh, I know all that. But I'm in a hurry. If we don't sign the contract today, this juicy deal will go to another company.'

It seemed like he hadn't consulted anyone else and was pursuing this deal on his own. But the head of Accounting was on a business trip in Kansai, so it would be impossible to get his seal by the end of the day.

'I'm sorry . . . but I really can't open the safe without a completed request form. If I break the rules, the chairman will be upset with me.'

'I'll let Dad know about it later. No matter what happens, I'll make sure there's no trouble for you.'

'Sorry, I can't do it.'

The head of Corporate Planning kicked over the waste basket near his foot. 'You're a rank-and-file twerp! Why are you acting so big? Just bring me the key!'

'Please stop. I can't do what I can't do.'

Hearing our voices, some other employees peeked into the room.

'If you won't give me the key, then I'll just take it.'

Business Cards

He shoved me aside and began ripping the drawers out of my desk and dumping their contents out.

'Where is it? Where'd you put it? Give me the key!'

He frantically searched every inch of the room – opening lockers and bookcase doors.

'I have the key, but I definitely can't give it to you.' I pulled the key hanging around my neck up to my collar to show him. It would be a mess if I lost it, so since the day the chairman entrusted it to me, I'd been keeping it on me.

Perhaps he realised people had gathered due to the growing commotion. He loudly clicked his tongue and spat, 'You'll pay for this' as a parting shot before leaving.

The relief only lasted an instant. Looking at the trashed office, I heaved a sigh. I had wanted to see a film on my way home from work, but it seemed like I would have to give up on that.

On the Monday of the next week, I was cleaning as usual when Maru-san came charging in to work.

'Hm? Good morning. You're awfully early.'

'Yeah, but given the situation, we're going to be terribly busy for a while.'

I didn't understand what he meant. 'The situation? Did something happen?'

Maru-san looked surprised and leaned in. 'Togawa-chan, didn't anyone tell you? The chairman passed away.'

'What . . .!'

Everything after that was such a whirlwind, I hardly remember anything. Before I knew it, I was seeing the hearse off to the crematorium.

Once the mourners had left the funeral venue, I returned to

begin cleaning up and my gaze met that of the portrait of the chairman on the altar. It felt like his eyes were telling me, *'That was rough, huh? Good work.'*

The next week, though we'd only just had the funeral, the new management structure was announced. Looking at the notice posted in the hall, I saw that the spot on the board of directors that opened with the chairman's passing had been filled by the head of Corporate Planning.

'He's an idiot of a son, but he must have inherited a bunch of stocks from his father.' Maru-san shook his head.

'Executive Director *and* head of Corporate Planning?! Has there ever been a director more likely to get swindled?!' Kaku-chan murmured, her face pale.

We had recently learned that the 'juicy deal' he wanted me to open the safe for was a scam. In other words, I had been right to adhere to the chairman's rules and keep the safe locked.

'More importantly, what'll happen to our jobs?'

The 'organisational restructuring outline' that had gone out with the HR notice said: *The General Affairs department will be abolished, and its functions will be shared among Accounting, HR and Corporate Planning.*

About a month after that, it was decided that I would be transferred to a small Sales office in the countryside, and we received notice that Maru-san and Kaku-chan's contracts would be terminated. Honestly, I wanted to complain, but I didn't know who to complain to.

'Well, we knew we only had jobs thanks to the chairman's kindness.'

Maru-san and Kaku-san seemed resigned and unsurprised;

Business Cards

they simply went about preparing things so that whoever took over their duties wouldn't struggle.

The day after I received my transfer orders, the head of General Affairs and HR called me in and took the key.

'It was only a few months, but you did well keeping a tight handle on it and preventing any mishaps. That said, even though it was on the chairman's orders, you went a bit overboard.'

'Are you talking about what happened with the head of Corporate Planning?'

The man who was supposedly my boss merely shrugged.

'Oh, about the cleaning of the road, who should I have take that over?'

Maybe he didn't know what I was talking about. At first, he gave me a strange look, but then he murmured, 'Oh, that,' in a low voice. 'You were just doing that because you felt like it, right? If someone wants to take it on, they can. Of course, it doesn't count as work for the company, so there's no overtime pay.'

I was so shocked, I didn't know what to say. I'd never once asked for extra compensation, either.

'Understood.' I bowed and was about to leave the HR office.

'Oh, and your "deputy supervisor" title won't count at your new office. The chairman forced it through as something you could use as long as you were in General Affairs. Make sure you return your business cards before you go.'

I didn't turn around.

We cleaned up the General Affairs office and handed all our duties over to the other departments. Once we were out, the office was slated to become a storage room. I never found someone to clean the road.

Notes from the Ginza Shihodo Stationery Shop

On Maru-san and Kaku-chan's last day at the office, we held a farewell for the General Affairs department at the restaurant where we'd eaten omuraisu with the chairman.

'I heard you'll be transferred to the countryside, Togawa-sama. And that your colleagues are retiring . . .' The manager's tone was concerned. There were only three of us at the table, but he had laid out a fourth napkin, knife and fork.

'I don't know when I'll be back in Tokyo, but I'm sure I'll have business trips, so I'll reach out. Let's meet here again.'

'Yes, I'll look forward to it.' Kaku-chan's cheerful tone was my only consolation.

'OK, time to drink. Togawa-chan, give us a word!' Maru-san picked up his glass.

'All right. Take care, you two. We need to make sure not to worry the chairman up in Heaven. Cheers!'

'Cheers!'

Suddenly, the candle on the table went out, despite a complete lack of wind. Through the rising wisp of smoke, I thought I could see the chairman sitting with us.

At the table on the landing at Shihodo, I propped my head up on my elbows and looked out of the window. At some point, it had started to rain. A woman in a trench coat with a bright red umbrella walked past. *Sure enough, any scene makes a pretty picture in Ginza*, I thought.

The thirty years after my first transfer I spent making a tour that impressively managed to only hit the small cities outside Tokyo. Along the way, I married a woman working at the office of a client, and we had three children, but work was always humdrum and there were no chances for promotion. Unfortunately, I

Business Cards

never ended up a section chief or head of a local office, the sort of position that would get you called to HQ for a meeting, so I had no business trips to Tokyo. Though we kept in touch through midsummer gifts and New Year's cards, I was never able to meet Maru-san or Kaku-chan again, and they both joined the dead long ago. And I heard that the restaurant where the manager was so nice to me closed when the bubble burst.

All the while, the company went through merger after merger, its name changing multiple times, until none of the chairman's family remained. Despite everything, I'm sure in part because the location was so good, the headquarters always remained in Ginza.

It was ten years ago that I returned to headquarters, assigned to a department with so much English in its name it felt like a tongue-twister: Corporate HQ Facility Management. The job ended up being no different from what I'd done in General Affairs.

The office was on a block that had been completely redeveloped. The gleaming building's lower floors were filled with shops, while luxury dining establishments occupied the uppermost floors; I knew if I cleaned the street on my own initiative, it would only bother people, so I refrained.

Instead, I did my best to greet everyone who frequented the building and learn their names. Curiously, it seemed as though when I energetically welcomed people, even those with severe expressions gradually opened their hearts to me.

When I glanced at my watch, I saw it had already been five minutes since I'd sat down. The rain was coming down even harder, and perhaps because of that, no one had come into the shop.

Notes from the Ginza Shihodo Stationery Shop

Takarada-san had waited patiently while I spaced out.

'Oh, sorry. I was just so comfortable here . . .' I rushed to my feet. 'I should be going.'

Takarada-san emphatically shook his head. 'No, look at that rain. Why don't you visit the first floor? There's a raised area with tatami, so you can take your shoes off and relax. Or if you'd like to read or write, there's a desk as well. Right this way.'

His extended arm indicated the stairs leading up to the first floor.

There were footlights at intervals on the stairs, but since no one was on the first floor it was pitch-dark. Once I arrived, finding my way using Takarada-san's back, I was caught off guard by the lights flashing on.

'Togawa-san, happy retirement!'

The shout came with the sound of a bunch of party poppers being let off.

Looking around the room, I saw over fifty people: Yamamoto-san, the security guard I always said hi to in the lobby; Matsumoto-san, who came to refill our vending machines; Furukawa-san, who was in charge of cleaning; Noda-san, who maintained the tea-dispensing machines; Tonomura-san, Mizukawa-san and Nanao-san from the reception desk; Marukawa-san from the post office, and Arita-san, who delivered packages; Chef Saito from the company canteen, as well as the staff cook Suzuki-san; plus many others who supported the company from behind the scenes.

'W-what are you all doing here?!' I could hardly speak. When I forced my voice out, it sounded funny, and everyone burst out laughing.

'What are we doing here? I think you know! You've been so

Business Cards

kind to all of us, so we wanted a chance to thank you, Togawa-san. As we were wondering what to do, Takarada-san was kind enough to suggest we use the first-floor space here. I put some feelers out, and before I knew it, we had this whole group of people,' said Yamamoto-san, the security guard.

Furukawa-san, the cleaner, continued, 'Togawa-san, you've always been so considerate. You always said hello and asked how we were. And you even worried sometimes, asking if we were struggling with anything. I don't really want to say it, but sometimes I feel a bit invisible. Some people pass by as if they don't realise I'm there, even though I'm cleaning right in front of them . . . But you were different, Togawa-san.'

'Sometimes we had plumbing issues in the kitchen, and while others would get angry and shout, "Hurry up and fix it!" you made phone calls for us and even started cleaning up the flooded floor with a bucket and rag. There's nobody else like you,' said Chef Saito, and Suzuki-san and the other canteen staffers nodded.

'But those things are all just common courtesy . . .' I had no more words.

'Hey, we were all waiting for you! Let's cheers already!' Matsumoto-san handed me a can of beer.

'This is a brand a company in our group makes. When I told the guys you were quitting at retirement age, everyone said, "Then please take these!" Really, they all wanted to come, but it was too many people, so I'm here as a representative.'

Everyone was looking at me so warmly. I truly had no words.

'Umm . . . thank you, everyone.'

That was all I could manage.

*

Notes from the Ginza Shihodo Stationery Shop

Yamamoto-san said a word and we drank. After that, I chatted for a while with everyone who had come. Really, I wanted to thank Takarada-san sooner, but the line of people waiting to talk to me was never-ending.

Maybe about an hour later, after we'd all managed to talk a bit, and people started to graze on the food that had been prepared, I was finally able to catch him.

'Err, thank you so much for everything.'

When I bowed my head, he said, flustered, 'None of that, please! It can't be good luck for me to make a customer feel like that! Besides, I hardly did anything . . . The others provided all the drinks and food. All I offered was to lead you up here.'

'I hardly think that's true! Really, thank you.' When I insisted on bowing, Takarada-san must have resigned himself, because he nodded.

'I helped a little, but it was because I was moved by how eager everyone was to have an opportunity to thank you. So I think it all comes down to your character, Togawa-sama.'

When I scanned the room, everyone seemed to be enjoying themselves.

'I'm glad . . . But really, everything is thanks to the one who patiently taught me how to be, back when I was an ignorant youngster,' I murmured, and Takarada-san nodded.

'So there's an old letterpress in the basement . . . During my predecessor's lifetime, we took various printing jobs, but it had been years since we'd operated it. I felt I had to do something about that, so I networked to find a specialist, got it overhauled and have been – slowly, but nevertheless – starting to print things like business cards. Anyhow, while I was organising the shelf next to the press, I found this.'

Business Cards

Takarada-san handed me a little plastic case. It appeared to have business cards inside.

'Are these . . .?'

Takarada-san nodded. 'It appears we had taken the order and ended up holding onto them. The last name is a bit uncommon, so I was wondering if maybe . . . Please go ahead and open the case.'

When I did as instructed, the postal code was three numbers shorter, and the phone number was one shorter, and of course there was no email address or mobile phone number – these were old business cards. The general design was the same as the 'Deputy Supervisor' ones I'd received from the chairman, but these said in sharp bold characters: SUPERVISOR.

'The box was stored with a copy of the order slip that had a note that said, "Ordered along with the Deputy Supervisor box." Apparently both types had been ordered at the same time.'

'. . . Chairman.'

I glanced out the window to find that the rain had stopped, and the moon was shining brightly in the cleared-up sky. It was just like a gentle smile from the chairman.

* * *

It was that time of year right before the big spring holiday period. The manager of the Ginza stationery shop Shihodo, Ken Takarada, was out on the street checking how the window display looked. Someone called out to him from behind.

'Hello, there!'

When Ken whirled around, his face broke into a smile. 'Well, if it isn't Togawa-sama! Irasshaimase.'

'It's been a little while, but I wanted to thank you again.'

Notes from the Ginza Shihodo Stationery Shop

'It was nothing.' As he replied, Ken looked curiously at Togawa. 'So, I don't mean to be rude, but didn't you retire? If you're in Ginza wearing a suit . . . does that mean you've started working again?'

Togawa smiled a bit sheepishly and then nodded. 'Yes, I don't have any hobbies aside from work, after all. I think I'd like to keep working while my body is able. But I got sick of being employed by other people, so I started my own company.'

'Your own company? Ohhh, I see. What kind of company is it?'

Togawa put on the grin of a mischievous child and asked, 'What's your guess?'

Ken thought for a little while, but eventually surrendered. 'I give up.'

'It's called General Affairs of Ginza.'

'General Affairs of Ginza?'

'Yes, because there are so many small businesses – restaurants, shops, you know. I created a company that can handle general affairs for all of them.'

'Ah-ha . . .' Ken nodded in what seemed to be admiration.

'And so . . . I'd like to make some business cards.'

'Oh, I'd be delighted to assist.'

Ken gently invited Togawa inside.

'What shall we do about your title? I think in this case it would probably be Representative Director and President, but . . .'

Togawa shook his head. 'No, I'd like you to make it Supervisor.'

'What? You're sure you don't want to be president?'

'Yes, I'm sure. I mean, it's hard to ask a president to do a

Business Cards

job for you, right? If I'm a supervisor, that makes it easy to consult with me while also allowing people to feel they can probably trust me.' He scratched the tip of his nose self-consciously.

'I see . . . Well, let's discuss the particulars of the design.'

'By all means. But I don't want anything too fancy!'

Here we are at the Ginza stationery shop Shihodo. It seems like the consultation between the shopkeeper and his client will take some time.

Bookmark

'I really am sorry,' Ken-chan said when the train started to move.

'I told you, I'm not mad.'

'Really, though? You seem kinda mad.'

Who wouldn't be . . .? I muttered in my head as I shifted my gaze out the window.

'I'll make it up to you soon, so please forgive me. Ryoko, are you listening?'

'Uh-huh.' I put the paperback I'd taken out of my Boston bag on my lap. 'It's not like we can control the weather. Anyway, you have a lot to do when we get back, so why don't you try to sleep a bit?'

'Well, yeah, but . . .'

I took one of the beers that we'd received from the innkeeper out of the paper bag sitting on the table at our seat, pulled the tab and handed it to Ken-chan.

'Here you go.'

'Err, sorry.' He bowed his head as he accepted the can.

'That's enough throwing your apologies in the bargain bin. Cheers.'

When I held out my can, he made his can touch it lightly.

'Cheers . . . Agh, I can't believe the blizzard of the decade had to happen *now*. I really don't get it.'

He glanced at me, and then tilted his can back.

'Who knows? I bring the sun everywhere I go, you know.'

Notes from the Ginza Shihodo Stationery Shop

'Mm, but I'm pretty sure the rain doesn't follow me around...' Ken grumbled.

I gave him a sidelong glance as I took a sip of my beer. It was properly chilled and – partly because the train car was well-heated – tasty. My mood lightened just a smidge. Come to think of it, this was the first time I'd been on a train for this long next to Ken-chan.

Not long ago, a regular at Shihodo who also came to our cafe now and then – Sho-chan – had given us a vacation as a present. Technically, he gave an accommodation voucher to Ken-chan and a travel voucher for transportation to me. Sho-chan's advice was to 'go as far away as you can', but for Ken-chan, who runs Shihodo on his own, the most he could manage was one night. In the end, we decided to go to an *onsen* area about three hours away by train.

The idea was that if we left on Wednesday, Shihodo's off day, and came back on the first train in the morning, he could be back by the time the shop would open, but while we were strolling around to see the sights after lunch, the weather took a turn.

In the evening, when we arrived at the inn, the woman running it was kind enough to inform us, 'It seems like the weather suddenly broke. They're saying there'll be a big snowstorm.' Though it was out of character for Ken-chan, he panicked.

'Oh nooo. I was going to open the shop tomorrow, so I didn't put up a note or anything to say we'd be closed.'

'It's OK. I'm sure my dad would put a note up if you asked him.'

My dad runs the cafe Hohozue, only a five-minute walk from Shihodo. Ken-chan and I have been friends since we were kids, so he's practically family; it didn't seem like it would be a big deal for him to ask my dad that favour.

'Plus, you could update the website, or tweet. There are all sorts of ways to announce an unexpected day off.'

'Yeah . . . that may be true, but . . .'

Ken-chan turned on the TV in the corner of the room and started looking for a news programme. He was working his phone in his right hand and the TV remote with the left – the dexterity.

'We came all this way, so why don't we go and get into the hot spring?'

The news was warning about the snowstorm with the caption: *Get ready for the low-pressure bomb!*

'Yeah, I guess you're right . . . We can soak first and think after.'

By the time we were out, snow was starting to flutter down around our inn.

'Umm, I'm really sorry, but I think I'm going to head home.'

'What?'

I was making tea at the low table wearing a *yukata* plus a padded kimono over it, but my hands froze.

'Now? We haven't even had dinner yet.'

'. . . Yeah, I know. The last train seems to be after ten, but by then the trains might be stopped due to the blizzard. Oh, you should stay, Ryoko. I'll be fine – I can get back on my own.'

I heaved a sigh in spite of myself. Ken-chan may have been fine, but I wasn't.

'I'm really sorry. But if I take the day off without announcing it in advance, some customers might worry. We have a lot of elderly customers, so announcing only online might not be enough. And I think a lot of people will be inconvenienced if I don't shovel around the shop. So . . . so, I really have to go.'

I knew this is how he is. He always thinks of others first and puts himself last.

'OK, I understand. Then let's go home.'

'Oh, no, you should stay, Ryoko.'

'I can't do that. If only you go back, it'll make it seem like we fought or something. I would hate that.'

I picked up the phone to call the desk.

When I told her we would be abruptly cancelling our stay and returning home, the innkeeper was surprised but handled everything promptly.

'We have a driver at the station, so I'll have him arrange your tickets. And we'll take you to the station in our car. Please wait while we get ready.'

After a short time, there was a call from the desk. When we got our stuff together and went down to the entrance, the innkeeper was waiting for us.

'What a pity about today. Please come again.'

When Ken-chan offered her the voucher, she said, 'I'll take this next time,' and refused to let us pay even though we were cancelling on the day of the reservation.

'But we soaked in the hot spring!'

Seeing us so flustered, she smiled and shook her head. 'We have no shortage of hot water! How could I let you pay when you haven't even experienced the dinner and breakfast service we're so proud of? Please do come again. I'll be waiting.'

Then she slowly, silently bowed her head. It was such a beautiful gesture, it made me think, *This is the kind of woman I want to be.*

'I realise it's more for you to carry, but please take this. There wasn't a lot of time, so it's not much, but my husband, the chef here, put together some things he'd like you to enjoy on the train.'

Inside the paper bag she handed us were two beers and two boxes of food.

'Thank you so much.'

We bowed.

'Goodness, please raise your heads. It can't be good luck for me to make customers feel like that!'

Ken-chan often said a similar line, so it was a little funny to see him looking so much obliged.

'Oh, excuse me. It's Gin-san calling.'

Vibrating phone in hand, Ken-chan went over to a corner of the lobby.

'It's really too bad, isn't it? I'm sure this was a precious chance for you . . .' the innkeeper whispered to me as I was left behind.

'Well, sort of . . .'

'But I'm sure things will be all right.' She gave me a firm nod and a smile.

'Hm? What things?'

'I have a sense that this will end up being a good memory.'

Somehow, I felt like her smile kind of saved me in that moment.

As if keeping pace with the accelerating train, the snow grew heavier and heavier.

'This does seem like it could be pretty bad.'

'. . . Yeah, I just hope we don't get stopped on our way.'

Usually Ken-chan was calm and I was the one feeling stressed, but on this day it seemed he couldn't relax. He must have been really worried about whether he would make it in time.

We both looked at the snow gliding by out of the window. At first, it was powdery, but before long the flakes were coming down in clumps that seemed almost as big as fingertips. Looking at our faces reflected in the glass, and the falling snow beyond, I remembered something similar that had happened a long time ago.

Looking down at the paperback in my lap, I saw my bookmark peeking out. Before I knew it, as I gazed between the bookmark and the falling snow, I found myself remembering events long past.

I first met Ken-chan in fourth grade.

'Ryoko-chan, this is my grandson. His name is Ken. He's ten, just like you, and he'll be going to your school starting from the second term this year. I'm sure he'll feel a bit lost, so I don't mean to put you out, but could you look after him? Thanks, I'm counting on you.'

In late August, when there was only a little of the summer holidays left, the old man from Shihodo Stationery brought Ken-chan over to the cafe.

When the old man introduced him, he bowed politely.

'Kensui-san, don't act like a stranger! Ken-chan, you can come over any time. Let us know if you ever need anything at all. I'll do whatever I can to help.'

There it is! Dad's lethal ability to make promises before considering whether he can keep them! I jabbed in my head. His kindness was one of his good points, but I was less than thrilled as the one who would actually be roped into trouble this time.

In the end, while Ken-chan's grandpa and my dad chatted over coffee, Ken-chan ate pudding in silence and then stared absent-mindedly at the road. He was very tame compared to the boys in my class. That was my first impression of him.

The next day on my way home from running an errand, I happened to pass by Shihodo and saw Ken-chan out front sweeping with a broom. Though it was still pretty early in the morning, the lingering summer heat was fierce, and there weren't many people on the streets.

'Morning.'

When I greeted him from behind, he whirled around with a start. But he didn't answer, just gave me a silent nod.

'Hey, when someone greets you, it's only polite to say one in return. C'mon, you have to say "Morning" back.'

I was picky about greetings – partially because my dad had hammered it into me that they were the foundation of customer service. And maybe because the customers at the cafe were all adults, I was pretty mature compared to all the other kids in my class – to the point that some of the boys called me 'Mum' or 'Ryoko the nag'.

'M-morning . . .' Ken-chan said softly after blinking a few times.

'Why so quiet? Did you eat a proper breakfast? If your grandpa can't make one for you, you can come over for a morning set. We open at seven.'

As I rattled all that off, Ken-chan leaned on his broom, listening.

'Got it?'

He was giving so little response that I started to worry if he was really listening.

'Yeah, I got it.'

Is this kid really the same age as me?

'Well, I'm running an errand, so I gotta go. Later.'

'Yeah, later.'

I remember thinking, *He talks like a literal parrot . . .*

When I got back to the cafe, Dad seemed free. The morning customers must have just left, and he had opened a newspaper. I told him I ran into Ken-chan outside Shihodo.

'He seems like kind of a wimp. Will he be able to survive?'

Dad lowered the paper a little and glanced at me before shaking his head. 'That's no way to talk, Ryoko. You know, Ken-chan . . . Well, never mind. At any rate, you're in the same year, so take good care of him.'

'Okaaay.'

The next day, I waited till the lunch customers left and went to the library to return the books I'd used to do my summer holiday homework. When I biked past Shihodo, I saw Ken-chan outside polishing the glass doors at the entrance.

I rang my bike's bell. 'Hello. What are you doing?'

Ken-chan turned around, and I saw he was sweating buckets.

'. . . Ryoko-chan. Err, I'm polishing the glass.'

I panicked a bit seeing how red his face was. I parked my bike and grabbed the water bottle I'd chucked in the basket. Whenever I went anywhere in the summer, even somewhere nearby, my dad always made me take a bottle full of cold barley tea, saying, *Drink before you get thirsty. You don't want heatstroke.* And in the summer, there were lots of people who showed up at the cafe feeling unwell. When that happened, he would have them drink plenty of water with a slice of lemon floating on top and give them a seat in line with the air conditioner. Ken-chan's red face made him look just like those customers.

I took the outer cap, which functioned as a cup, off the flask, poured tea into it and handed it to Ken-chan.

'Here, hurry up and drink this.'

Ken-chan accepted the cup with two hands and drank it down with audible gulps. When I refilled the empty cup, he inhaled that in no time, too.

'Thanks, that was good.'

I had the feeling his face was looking a little more normal.

'Who in their right mind is out polishing glass in the middle of a summer day? What'll you do if you get heatstroke! You gotta be careful!'

'Yeah . . . but it was dirty.'

I heaved a sigh in spite of myself.

'You were sweeping yesterday, and today you're polishing. Are you spending all your time cleaning?'

Ken-chan blinked. The way his eyes looked when he did it was kind of cute, like a puppy's. 'Well, mostly . . .'

'Did the owner tell you to help?'

Ken-chan shook his head. 'No. No, but . . . he gives me a place to sleep and feeds me, does all sorts of things for me, so I feel like I should do something in return. But I don't know anything about how the shop works, so just about all I can do is clean.'

It was my first time having a real conversation with him, and I was kind of surprised. *He can actually talk!*

'But he's your grandpa, right?! It's only natural that he would take care of you. Oh, but where are your mum and dad?'

Notes from the Ginza Shihodo Stationery Shop

'Dad travels a lot for work. Mum died a long time ago. That's why I ended up living here with my grandpa.'

'... Oh.' I suddenly felt bad. It was like I'd forced him to answer a question that shouldn't have been asked.

'Sorry, but I want to finish this. Thanks for the tea. It was good. Later.'

With that, he went back to polishing the glass. As I watched more closely, I could see the motions of his hands were practised. It didn't seem at all like the work of a fourth-grader.

'OK, yeah, see you ... Oh, but you should take it easy on hot days.'

Ken-chan gave me a slight nod and continued polishing the glass.

The next day, when things at the cafe slowed down, I went over to Shihodo. As expected, Ken-chan was out scrubbing the stone steps at the entrance with a deck brush. I noticed a water bottle standing in a shady corner. *So he learned to be a bit more mindful*, I thought, and went back to Hohozue without talking to him.

I was curious, so I stopped by again the next day, and sure enough, he was cleaning the road. After a week of that, Shihodo's exterior was so pristine, it almost looked like a different shop.

On the last day of the summer holiday, when I passed by Shihodo, Ken-chan was using a rag to wipe down the red, cylindrical postbox in front of the shop.

'You finally ran out of things to clean, so you're polishing the postbox?' I laughed, and Ken-chan scratched the back of his head self-consciously.

'No, that's not why ... This thing is here smiling with its mouth open every day no matter what, whether it's hot, rainy, windy . . . I kind of felt like he was cheering me on while I was cleaning. It was a little dirty, so I felt like wiping it down. I don't have any friends, so . . .'

'I see . . . Oh, but if you have no friends, that means you're not counting me as a friend!'

Ken-chan's eyes went as wide as the first day I'd spoken to him.

'Are we friends?'

'Are we not?'

Ken-chan thought for a little while. 'If you say we're friends, then we must be friends.'

'What's that supposed to mean?'

It was so goofy, I laughed.

That night, I told my dad about our exchange. He listened in silence, polishing glasses at the counter, and then looked me square in the eye and said, 'Listen to me. And never speak a word of anything I'm about to say to anyone else. Understand?' Usually he was full of jokes, but now his face was terribly serious. 'Ken-chan's father is an amazingly talented landscape painter. He makes diaphanous watercolours, as well as the original art for *shin-hanga* – you know he's the real deal when you see his work. Go to any library, and they'll have a collection of his art; that's how famous he is.'

'A landscape artist . . . So that's why he travels all the time.'

Dad nodded. 'His name is Bokushu Takarada. According to Kensui-san, up until this July, Ken-chan and his dad were travelling all across Japan together. Apparently when he finds a subject that piques his interest, he sits right down and begins to paint. It might take as long as several months, or it could be as short as just a few weeks, and then he's off to the next place.

Notes from the Ginza Shihodo Stationery Shop

That's why Ken-chan doesn't have anyone he can call a friend – he's been constantly changing schools.'

'Oh . . .' I felt like I sort of understood what Ken-chan had been saying.

'When he finishes a piece, he sends it to the dealer he's contracted with, and the payment gets used up on supplies and travelling in search of his next subject. He's famous in the art world, but it's not as if he's a household name, so it must have been a hard life. I'm sure there were fans of his art who were kind enough to put them up at times . . . I heard that Ken-chan would always make an effort to do something in return, like cleaning or laundry, tidying up . . . Kensui-san was telling me that Ken-chan has always paid close attention to the moods of the adults around him and taken pains to be considerate. It's a bit sad, isn't it? This is the period of his life he should be enjoying the freedom of being a child the most . . .'

'Does that mean he won't be here very long, either?'

Dad shook his head. 'No, apparently Bokushu declared that he wanted to go to foreign lands in search of unfamiliar subjects. He couldn't very well take a kid overseas, so he left him with Kensui-san at Shihodo.'

'Ah.' That was kind of a relief. 'Oh, but Ken-chan said his mum died. So his family is just like ours?'

My mum had died not long after giving birth to me, so I had no memories of her.

'Mm, yeah.'

Dad came out from behind the counter, went over to the record rack and used a stepping stool to pull an album off the top shelf. On the cover, a pretty woman was posing in front of a piano.

'Ken-chan's mother, Lilly Aikawa, was a jazz singer who put out several albums, but she passed away due to an illness five years ago.'

As Dad spoke, he put the record on the player. A moment later, her singing voice came over the speakers.

'It must have been hard to lose his mum when he was five . . .'

'. . . Coming from you, it has a different impact.'

'I'm fine. I mean, I don't even remember anything about Mum . . .'

Dad said nothing and just stared at the record going around.

At some point, the train had slowed down.

'This is an announcement for passengers. Due to high winds, we will cross the upcoming bridge at low speed. As a result, arrivals at each station will be between ten and thirty minutes delayed. There may be additional delays along our way due to the snow. We're terribly sorry but thank you for your understanding.'

Maybe due to the strain of an unusual situation, the conductor was speaking rapidly.

'I wonder if we'll actually make it back to Tokyo . . .' This kind of nervous murmur was out of character for Ken-chan.

'Stressing out about it won't help. Why don't we eat the bento the innkeeper gave us?'

I took the boxes of food out of the paper bag and handed one to Ken-chan.

'Yeah . . . I guess.'

'If the snow is bad enough to stop this train, you won't have any customers tomorrow, anyhow. C'mon, less worrying, more eating.'

Notes from the Ginza Shihodo Stationery Shop

When we unwrapped the boxes and opened them up, our voices overlapped.

'This is fantastic . . .!'

'Wow, looks delicious!'

We glanced at each other without really meaning to.

Inside the boxes were shrimp, smelt, sweet potato, maitake mushroom and shishito pepper tempura; sautéed salmon with cream sauce, spinach and shimeji mushrooms; simmered eel, daikon radish, carrot and satoimo with courgette and pea pods for a splash of colour; diced steak with grilled vegetables; little barrel-shaped rice balls sprinkled with sesame seeds and shredded shiso; and there was melon and strawberries for dessert.

The moment we snapped our chopsticks apart, Ken-chan dug in at his usual breakneck speed.

'Ahh, you don't have to rush so much. No one is coming to steal your food!'

Before I knew it, I was saying my usual line. Come to think of it, the first time I said it to him was back in those early days.

On 1 September, the second term began. I left Hohozue a little earlier than usual and headed for Shihodo. Shihodo is only five minutes from Hohozue, but it was in the opposite direction from school, so, to be honest, this was kind of annoying.

When I pressed the intercom button at the side door, Ken-chan's grandpa's voice eventually said, 'Hello?'

'It's Ryoko. Good morning. I came to pick up Ken-chan. I thought we could go to school together.'

'Ohh, right. Is it already that time?'

Bookmark

The intercom clicked off in the rush of the moment.

I must have waited about five minutes. Finally, the pair of them came out.

'What about your *randoseru*?' I asked.

Ken-chan responded by holding up a day pack. 'This is all I have.'

'Oh, huh. OK.' It was pretty rare for elementary schoolers to use a regular backpack, so it caught me off guard. I addressed Ken-chan's grandpa, who was standing there absent-mindedly behind him. 'Are you coming with us?'

'No, I went to fill out the transfer paperwork last week and they said he could just show up.'

'Oh, but today is only the ceremony for the start of the new term, so there's no lunch. We'll be back before noon.'

He looked troubled. 'Ohhh, I thought for sure there would be lunch. Sorry, Ken, but please stop by Hohozue and have something on your way home. I'm busy today so I won't be able to prepare anything.'

Most of Hohozue's regulars had tabs. Of course, Ken-chan's grandpa was a regular, so anything Ken-chan ate or drank could go on his tab.

Ken-chan nodded silently and then followed after me.

When we got to school, it turned out Ken-chan was put in the same class as me. Maybe the teacher was being considerate of his grandpa, given the situation.

The whole school was interested in Ken-chan – even the kids from the older grades stopped by to get a look at him. A transfer student had come to our tiny, little elementary school with only two classes to a grade and about 300 kids in total, so it was no wonder everyone was excited.

Notes from the Ginza Shihodo Stationery Shop

'Hey, Ryoko. You came to school with the new kid, right? Do you know him?' my classmate Chihiro whispered in my ear.

'He just lives in my neighbourhood. The manager at Shihodo asked me to take care of him . . . He's a regular at the cafe, so I couldn't very well turn him down . . .'

'Oh, huh. But I'm kinda jealous! Isn't he cute?'

I shook my head at Chihiro's grown-up-sounding comment.

That day, after taking care of a few things, like turning in our summer holiday homework and deciding who would be in charge of different events during the second term, we went home; it was just before eleven. I went back to Hohozue with Ken-chan and sat him at the end of the counter.

It was eleven-thirty, so the lunch rush was about to begin. I gave Ken-chan the menu and then brought him a glass of water and a wet hand towel.

'What do you want to eat? Pick something from the list.' As I spoke, I put on my apron and tied a bandana around my head so that it covered my hair. Ken-chan took a sip of water before carefully reading each item on the menu down the line. All the while, customer after customer came in, and I worked as usual: seating them, serving water, taking orders.

Ten minutes must have passed. When I went back to Ken-chan, he was still reading the menu.

'Did you decide?'

When I spoke to him, he looked up in surprise. 'There are a lot of choices . . .'

'You think so? It seems like a pretty normal cafe menu to me. So what'll you have?'

Ken-chan said, 'Toast,' still looking at the menu.

'What? You mean plain toast? Are you sure that's all you want?!'
'... Yeah.'
'Why? How about trying something a little more substantial...? Like, we have all sorts of stuff.'

Plenty of people order a toast set in the morning, but it was my first time seeing someone order toast à la carte for lunch.

Dad noticed our exchange and interrupted. 'What, are you thinking about money? Don't worry. I got a call from your grandpa, and he said to give you whatever you wanted. He'll pay the tab at the end of the month, so you can relax and order anything you like.'

At Dad's words, Ken-chan blinked and went back to studying the menu.

When I passed by him a little while later, he quietly asked, 'Is there something you recommend?'

'Hmm, if you're not that hungry, how about pizza toast? If you want to eat a proper meal, then the Naporitan spaghetti, Hayashi rice or omuraisu are all tasty.'

'Then I'll have the pizza toast.'

'Huh? Oh, OK. Pizza toast, then.'

Ken-chan nodded at me.

I wrote 'Pizza T 1' on an order slip, washed my hands and took out the bread. I cut a slice about three centimetres thick.

'What? You're gonna make it?!' Ken-chan leaned over the counter in surprise.

'Yeah. I'm in charge of the easy stuff like toast, sandwiches and hot dogs. Dad won't let me make stuff like spaghetti or omuraisu that uses the stove yet.'

I spread tomato sauce on the piece of bread, sprinkled some

minced onion and then added plenty of shredded cheese. After topping that with green pepper and salami, I sprinkled more cheese and then popped it into the toaster oven.

With my hands free, I grabbed a side salad I'd prepared ahead of time out of the fridge and gave it to Ken-chan along with a fork.

'Wow . . . I'm kinda surprised.'

His admiring tone made me happy. 'Oh, yeah? It's not that big a deal. Oh, the set comes with a drink. What sounds good? Hot coffee or tea, or if you want something cold there's iced coffee or tea, or you could have milk or orange juice.'

'Then I'll have orange juice.'

I couldn't help but laugh. 'A kid drink, huh? Are you sure you don't want iced coffee?'

'Mmm . . . I've never had coffee before.'

'What? Seriously? Then by all means stay in your comfort zone and drink orange juice.' I put on big sister airs and served him orange juice.

That happened to be the end of the carton, so I rinsed it out and was about to throw it in the bin when Ken-chan said, 'Oh!'

'What?'

'Are you throwing that away?'

'Yeah, it's empty.' I showed him the inside through the opening.

'. . . Then, could I have it?'

'Sure, but what are you going to do with it?'

'Use it for papermaking.'

'Papermaking? What's that?' I asked without thinking, and Ken-chan's face said, *Huh?*

'It's, uh ... making paper.'

'Wow, you can make your own paper?' As I answered, I dried the carton off and handed it to Ken-chan.

'Thanks.' He bowed his head politely, even though I'd only given him something I was going to throw away anyway.

'Don't do that! If you want cartons, we have a ton of them. We're using them every day. Milk cartons, cream cartons ...'

'You throw them all away?'

'Yeah.'

'That's such a waste ...' The tone of his voice made it clear he felt it from the bottom of his heart.

'Will you take them if I save them for you?'

'Yeah, of course.'

Ken-chan's face lit up and at the same moment, the toaster dinged.

Taking care not to burn myself, I took the toast out, cut it into rough quarters, set it on a plate I'd put a napkin on and served it to Ken-chan.

'Here you go. Sorry for the wait. It's hot, so be careful.'

Before I could even finish, Ken-chan bowed his head to say, 'Itadakimasu!' and chomped into the pizza toast.

'Ow, it's hot! A-and good!' He blinked in shock.

'Ahh, you don't have to rush so much. No one is coming to steal your food!' I couldn't help but comment. Ken-chan nodded but continued eating at the same speed.

I'd made pizza toast a zillion times, but I'd never seen anyone eat it with such relish as Ken-chan was. To be honest, it made me really happy.

After polishing off the pizza toast in less than three minutes, Ken-chan fixed his eyes on me and nodded. 'That was really good, thanks. I think it's the first time in my life I've ever eaten anything that tasty . . . You're amazing.'

He said it with a straight face, and though I wasn't the type to blush, I sure did in that moment.

'That's a bit overkill . . .'

Every now and then, there are times I wish I could just say 'Thank you'.

The next day, and for a while afterwards, the two of us went to school together, but, eventually, Ken-chan made friends with some boys, and we started going separately.

Still, on Saturdays when there was no lunch served at school, he would come by Hohozue to eat on his way back to Shihodo. He ordered pizza toast every time.

'Don't you get sick of it?' I asked.

'Nope, not at all.' He was almost stubborn in his determination to eat pizza toast.

In the end, he ate it for about three months, before abruptly trying a hot dog one day and switching to that for the next three months . . . That's how he is; I'm pretty sure he still hasn't tried everything on the menu.

Every time he came to our place, he went home carrying the empty cartons I'd saved for him as if they were treasure.

'Do you really have a use for so many cartons? You're not just throwing them away at home, are you?'

'No, of course not . . . I'm really using them. I give them a good soak in water, then peel the film off and mix it so the paper fibres come apart. Once it's all pulpy, I add a little paste and then use a papermaking mould to scoop the mixture up. After the sheets are dry, I can use them for doodling or writing.'

'Oh, huh. Then can I have some too?'

Ken-chan blinked and then looked at me. 'Yeah, sure. Got it. I'll definitely give you some.'

In the end, Ken-chan spent about fifteen minutes eating the bento as the train pummelled through the thickening snow. Though he must have been worrying about the weather as he nursed his can of beer, I could tell that he was trying to be considerate of me in his own way.

When I finished eating about ten minutes later, Ken-chan stood up with his phone and said, 'I'll go throw away the rubbish. While I'm up, I'll give your dad a call and see what the snow's like there.'

'Oh, then do you want me to call?'

'No, it's OK. He might not answer if he's outside salting the road, anyhow. In that case, I'll try calling someone else from the shop association.'

There are over ten shop associations in Ginza, and Shihodo and Hohozue are in the same one. A few years back, Ken-chan was nominated to be chair. Thanks to juggling that extra role, he seems to have got to know a lot more of the business managers on the street.

'Anyhow, I'll be right back.'

Watching Ken-chan make his way down the aisle with the rubbish, I recalled Observation Day.

The second term of fourth grade was halfway over in the blink of an eye. Then came Culture Day in November. At the school we attended, Culture Day was observed by holding a kind of open house – essentially it was an observation day for parents and guardians. Though the era had passed from Showa to Heisei, most of the guardians who showed up were mothers; it was still rare for a father or grandfather to put in an appearance. For that reason, I hated Observation Day. I was happy Dad came, of course, but having a male relative in attendance made you stand out. I was jealous of classmates who had mothers who would go to a salon to get their hair done and show up in a stylish outfit. Still, I knew Dad looked forward to Observation Day, so I could never tell him not to come.

That year, our class ended up being observed for Japanese class, and my dad came along with Ken-chan's grandpa. As expected, it was mostly mothers again, so the two men stuck out.

Before the start of class, a troublemaker turned around and then rudely murmured, 'There are two old dudes mixed in with all the ladies!' All the boys snickered.

Then another kid said, 'No, it's an old dude and a grandpa!'

Unable to talk back to all the boys, I just hung my head – even though I knew Dad would be happy if I turned around and waved.

Ken-chan glanced at me from the next seat over and then stood up and headed to the back where the grown-ups were standing. I whirled around in a panic and said, 'Hey!' but it was too late.

Once he had approached his grandpa, he said in a clear voice, loud enough for everyone to hear: 'Grandpa, thanks for coming today even though the shop is so busy,' and then, 'I'll do my best in class.' His grandpa nodded and murmured a vague reply. The troublemaker and his friends seemed lost for a response.

When I looked up, I saw my dad standing next to Ken-chan's grandpa, and our eyes met. He mouthed, 'Do your best,

Ryoko,' and I gave him a little nod. Just then, the teacher came in and the chime sounded.

That day in Japanese class, we were presenting poems. The previous week, we'd learned some basic poetry-writing skills. As homework, we were told to choose either 'school', 'friends' or 'family' as a theme and write a poem for this day.

Honestly, I had no idea what to write for my poem, and I put off thinking about it for ages. In the end, I had brute-forced my way through the assignment the night before, choosing 'school' and stringing together some memories of my life at school so far in a 'poetic' way. It definitely wasn't the sort of thing I felt I could read in front of everyone.

'So who would like to read their poem?' asked our teacher, scanning the room.

As nearly everyone lowered their eyes, one hand went up.

'I would!'

'Great, then you're up, Takarada-kun.'

I looked over at Ken-chan in surprise. His face looked more solemn than I'd ever seen it before.

Maybe he noticed me looking. He glanced over, gave me a little nod, then stood up, grabbed his folded sheet of composition paper and walked up to the front of the classroom. He stood so straight, and the atmosphere around him was so dignified, he almost seemed like a different kid.

He stood in front of the blackboard.

'OK, Takarada-kun. Your theme was "friends", right?'

Ken-chan nodded and unfolded his paper.

'You think you're so cool, huh, Takarada?!' jeered the troublemaker, and a few of the boys laughed. Some of the mothers began whispering to each other.

Notes from the Ginza Shihodo Stationery Shop

'All right, quiet please.' When the teacher admonished them, the room fell silent. 'You can start when you're ready.'

Ken-chan nodded firmly, then took a deep breath and began to read aloud.

Friends
By Ken Takarada

Ever since birth I've been alone
but I've never been lonely

Ever since birth I've been travelling
north for spring and summer, south for autumn
    and winter
I'm sure I've seen so many amazing sights, but I can't
    remember a thing
I've been alone

I've always wondered why I can't remember anything
but recently I solved the puzzle
I can't remember because I was alone

This summer I arrived in Tokyo
It's cluttered and not a pretty place
but I was able to make lots of memories

From now on, I want to continue making memories
with the friend who reached out to me
when I was alone

*

His voice reverberated strongly in my heart. Before I knew it, I was clapping. The applause grew until it enveloped the entire classroom.

That night, Dad closed the cafe early and invited Ken-chan and his grandpa over for dinner. He put his cooking skills on full display to prepare a feast for us. I'll say it even as his daughter – it was truly delicious. Dad and Ken-chan's grandpa must have been having fun – they were both in high spirits, and they drank a lot.

Leaving them to their party, Ken-chan and I went to my room.

'Wow, you have your own room, huh.' The moment we stepped inside, he looked around curiously.

'You don't? It seems like there would be a lot of rooms above the shop.'

He shook his head lightly. 'There are a lot of rooms, but there's a lot of stuff in them – inventory for the shop and whatnot – maybe, like, accounting books? – so I don't have a room.'

'Oh . . .'

I offered the seat at my desk to Ken-chan and sat down on a floor cushion.

'Your poem today was really good.'

'Thanks . . .' He smiled bashfully.

'How did you come up with something so good?'

I was kind of curious.

'. . . I don't really know "how", but . . .'

'But?'

'We talked in front of the postbox one day, right? I just wrote down exactly what I felt that day.'

My heart filled with some kind of happy but also embarrassed emotion I didn't really understand.

'But you can write so well just like that? Are you sure you don't write poetry in your spare time?' I pressed him for details to gloss over how flustered I was.

'Mm . . . Well, I've never really told anyone this before, but when I find a poem I like, I copy it in my own handwriting.'

'Huh?'

The conversation went in a totally unexpected direction, so I felt a bit bewildered.

In lieu of a reply, Ken-chan took a little diary out of his pocket. It was black and had a thin pencil slipped in near the spine. The words *Jet-ace MEMORIAL BOOK* were on the cover in gold letters; it didn't seem at all like the sort of thing an elementary schooler would carry around.

'Until not that long ago, I was wandering all around Japan with my dad. He's a painter who specialises in landscapes, so we were always going to *fukomeibi* spots. Usually there would be a signboard with some kind of explanation.'

'Huh . . .' I'd never heard a ten-year-old use a four-kanji compound to say 'scenic' before. Sometimes I wasn't sure whether Ken-chan was mature or childish . . .

'Those signs often have a poem, like a haiku or whatever style, written by a local poet. So if I read it and thought, "Oh, I like that," then I would copy it down. Because if you only read it once, you'll definitely forget it, right? And you may not be able to return to that spot again . . .'

I took the diary when he offered it to me.

'It's OK for me to look?'

Ken-chan silently nodded.

I opened it to find detailed notes in neat handwriting. There were different types of poems – haiku, tanka and so on –

and below each one he'd written notes, such as where he found it, the date and the poet's name. A quick flip through revealed there were about fifty poems.

'This is kind of impressive. Are you really a fourth-grader, Ken-chan?'

He shook his head with a blank expression. 'There's nothing impressive about it! I just copied what I saw. It's easy.'

Suddenly, I felt like such a kid – so embarrassed.

I hurriedly grabbed a record leaning against a corner of my bookshelf.

'Ta-da! Here's a present from me. Your poem was good today, so I'll play this record for you.'

It was the Lilly Aikawa album Dad had showed me.

'Who's that?'

'Huh? You don't know?'

That was a bit of a surprise.

'Nope . . . She's pretty, though.'

'Dad told me she was your mum . . .'

'. . . Oh.'

Suddenly, I started feeling like I was doing something really cruel.

'Sorry . . . I thought you would know.'

Ken-chan took the album from my hands and stared at it.

'The face I remember was much thinner . . . And I never saw her wearing this much make-up. But, on closer look, yeah, I can tell it's her.'

'Err, I'm really sorry. That was weird. Maybe it was inconsiderate.'

Ken-chan slowly shook his head. 'Not at all. It seems like it's painful for Dad to remember, so he never tells me anything.

Notes from the Ginza Shihodo Stationery Shop

But I have been thinking I'd like to learn more about my mum. What about you, Ryoko-chan? Grandpa told me you lost your mum when you were even smaller than me.'

'... My mum died right after I was born, so I don't know anything about her. Everything I think I know is just what Dad has told me. They met, had a grand romance and got married, and then I was born ... And then she died. I've heard the story over and over, so I'm convinced it must be the truth ... but I bet Dad is determined not to upset me, so he probably made up a bunch of things.'

'Hmm ... But I wonder which is better: hearing nothing like me or getting told all kinds of stuff like you.'

'I wonder ...'

Ken-chan held the album out to me. 'Can we listen to it?'

'Yeah, of course. That's why I have it here.'

'Then play it for me!' He peered into my face.

'Sure, but ... are you sure you want to hear it?'

'Yes.'

I took the album out of Ken-chan's hands. I powered up my ladybird-shaped portable record player, put the record on it and dropped the needle.

After a moment, there was some quiet piano. A woman's voice glided in to complement the melody. Her voice and the piano seemed to whisper to each other for a little while, and then at some point, a bass and drums began to keep time.

The lyrics seemed to be mostly English, but now and then some Japanese was mixed in, which created a unique tenderness.

After thirty minutes, the A side ended. Ken-chan had leaned back in the chair and was gazing absent-mindedly out the window.

I flipped the record to the B side in silence. This side seemed to be a live recording, and the murmuring presence of the crowd, applause and whistles remained between songs.

'So this is my mum's voice.'

'Is it different from what you remember?'

'Hmm . . . I'm not sure. Speaking voices and singing voices are different, after all. Plus it's jazz, I guess? And the lyrics were in English or something.'

'I see . . .'

I flipped the record player off.

'Thanks for the wonderful present. I feel happy, almost like my mum was telling me what a good job I did today.'

Ken-chan stood up from my chair and bowed.

'Ah, don't do that. I'm regretting being such a busybody . . . Oh, I know. I'll lend it to you. You can take it home if you want. It actually belongs to the cafe, but I'm sure Dad'll say it's fine, too.'

I took the record off the player, put it in its jacket and held it out to Ken-chan.

'No, it's OK. At Grandpa's house we have a little tape player, but no record player. And I don't own a single record, so I'm not sure I would know where to keep it. Plus, now I know it's at Hohozue, so if I want to listen to it, I'll just stop by.'

'Are you sure?'

'Yeah.'

After that, we went downstairs to the cafe to find Dad and his grandpa plastered. Ken-chan skilfully helped his grandpa up and supported him as they set off walking.

'Are you going to be OK? You could just let him sleep here, no need to force it.'

Ken-chan shook his head. 'I'm used to this from my dad, so it's OK. And Shihodo is right over there . . . Well, good night.'

'Good night.'

I left the cafe and watched the pair of them receding unsteadily until they turned the corner.

When I peeked into the cafe, Dad must have gone upstairs after using the bathroom, because it was empty. I went to my room to get the album and then returned to set it on the cafe's turntable. Really, I wish I could've burned a CD, but Hohozue's audio system was old and could only dub cassettes. I unwrapped one of the blank tapes Dad kept on hand, put it in the deck, dropped the needle on the record and softly hit REC.

'Sounds like it started snowing in Tokyo, too.' As soon as he got back to his seat, Ken-chan heaved a sigh. The train was still moving slowly, and we hadn't even reached the first scheduled stop yet.

'We're already an hour delayed, huh?'

'Yeah . . . If this was how it was going to be, I shouldn't have forced it.'

It was rare for him to voice regrets.

'What are you talking about? It's way too late for that. There's no point in stressing out now.'

He glanced at me before grumbling, 'Aghhh . . .' and crossing his legs and closing his eyes.

'Yes, that's right. Relax and get some sleep.'

I picked up the paperback from my lap and looked again at the bookmark just barely peeking out. I'd been doing my best to take care of it, but it had got so old.

*

Bookmark

I thought the poem Ken-chan read on Observation Day was great, but it was a different kid's poem that got submitted to the prefecture's poetry contest. We heard later that his wasn't selected because it was so mature-sounding that people felt it didn't have any elementary-schooler charm.

'That's the worst!' I thought it was an outrage, but Ken-chan just shrugged.

'It is what it is. You liked it, so I'm satisfied with that.'

The term continued on with our social studies field trip, the tug-of-war competition between classes and so on. With each event he participated in, Ken-chan fit into the class better and better; he even got along with the troublemakers well enough to kick a football around or play baseball together.

Before I knew it, Christmas Eve was upon us. Like every year, Hohozue took Christmas cake orders from regulars. The deadline to order is about a week ahead of time, and we close early on 23 December to start baking.

Dad and I worked frantically, finally finishing the last of them around the time the date changed over. When I glanced outside, I saw snow was falling.

'Look! It's snowing!'

'Oh, so we'll have a white Christmas ... But I hope it doesn't stick. Shovelling is a lot of work, you know? And, on top of that, we don't get as many customers.'

'Oh, c'mon, it's gonna be a romantic Christmas and that's all you can say?'

When I pouted, Dad gave me a curious look. 'You're not saying you have a boyfriend or something, right?'

'What?! N-no way.' My voice cracked and even I had to admit I had reacted weirdly.

Notes from the Ginza Shihodo Stationery Shop

'Come to think of it, you were writing a note and doing some wrapping, right? Who was that for? It couldn't be a boy, right? Someone I know?'

'No, no! It's not like that!'

I ran off to my room, flustered.

Then it was morning. The snow had only piled up a little bit, but it continued to fall on and off.

From the moment the cafe opened, customers came through one after the other to pick up the cakes they had ordered, but there was no sign of Ken-chan's grandpa. I thought Ken-chan might come instead, but that didn't happen, either.

'Did they forget? Should I go and deliver it?'

Dad shook his head. 'No need to panic. There's still time before we close. I'm sure they have their reasons, so just wait. It's a busy period for Shihodo, too, you know. Lots of grown-ups give fountain pens, high-class ballpoint pens, imported organisers and whatnot as Christmas presents. And I think there are quite a few people who come in at the last minute ordering *nengajo* for New Year's. If you go to deliver it without being asked, it'll only cause trouble.'

I knew he was right, but I couldn't help but worry about their cake.

In the afternoon, a steady stream of customers meeting up for Christmas dates came in, and we were so busy, my head was spinning. Generally, one half of a couple would show up about ten minutes early, and once the other showed up, they would leave almost right away, so there were always new people coming in.

The snow really started coming down in the evening, and there was already about five centimetres on the ground. Huddled together, determined not to slip, all the people disappearing into the streets of Ginza seemed filled with happiness; they were enjoying their special date in a special place.

'Hey, Dad. Where should someone like me, who was born and grew up in Ginza, go on a Christmas date?'

He replied unenthusiastically. 'It's about ten years too soon for you to be thinking about that.'

Before I knew it, there were only ten minutes left until closing time. When I heard the door open, I called out, 'Irasshaimase!' by habit, only to find Ken-chan standing there. He was carrying an umbrella, but the wind was so strong, the duffel coat he was wearing was white with snow.

'Umm, I came for this.' He held out the cake voucher we gave to customers at the time of their order.

'I thought you were never gonna come!' I took out the last cake box that was in the fridge.

'Sorry, I had planned to come earlier, but . . . between wrapping presents and delivering the nengajo we printed, it was already evening. Then, just as I was about to go, the snow had started piling up, so Grandpa asked me to shovel . . .'

So Dad was right. I sighed in spite of myself.

'Anyhow, you made it! Phew. Next year if you can't find time to come, give us a call and I'll bring it over.'

'Huh? You do deliveries?'

I had the feeling it had been a while since I'd seen him blink in surprise like that.

'Not for just anyone! Regulars are special.' I put the cake in a bag and came out from around the counter to hand it to Ken-chan. 'Here you go. One Hohozue Christmas cake. It doesn't have any preservatives or anything in it, so finish it off by around noon tomorrow at the latest.' I imitated Dad's explanation.

'OK, thanks. We'll eat it after dinner.'

Ken-chan accepted the bag with one hand and took something out of his coat pocket with his free hand. It was a little envelope.

'Umm, this is for you . . . if you want it.'

I took the envelope when he offered it. 'What is it?'

'. . . A Christmas present. But I've never given anyone a present before, so I had no idea what you'd like. It might not be what you're expecting . . .'

'Thanks . . . So, can I open it?'

'Sure.'

I used the scissors at the till to cut open the envelope. There was a bookmark inside.

'Ooh . . .'

It was handmade washi with some thickness to it and a pale blue marble pattern painted on it; a navy ribbon was threaded through a hole in one spot. In the corner, there was a handwritten label: *K to R*.

'It's pretty. A bookmark?'

Ken-chan nodded. 'Because it seems like you go to the library pretty often . . . I thought you might use it.'

I didn't think he was interested in me at all, so that was a surprise.

'You know the paper cartons you always give me? I used those to make the washi and then used a technique called *suminagashi* to add the pattern.'

'You made this?!'

Ken-chan grinned. 'I promised I'd give you something I made with the cartons, right?'

'You remembered . . .'

Bookmark

The fact that he hadn't forgotten my casual request made me happy.

Ken-chan scratched the back of his head self-consciously and then turned on his heel to go with a 'Well, later'.

'Oh, wait a sec!'

I took a little package out of the drawer by the till.

'It's not like a thank you or something . . . umm . . . Merry Christmas.'

'Huh? You got me a present?' Ken-chan asked as he accepted the package.

'Well, kind of.'

Ken-chan smiled slightly in a nervous, self-conscious way. 'Thanks . . . I wonder what it is. Can I open it?'

'Of course.'

I held the cake bag for him. Ken-chan neatly undid the ribbon and paper.

'This is a cassette tape, right?'

'Yeah, you said you have a tape player, right? So I made a copy of the album we listened to together for you.'

'. . . Thanks. So you can copy records to tapes, huh?'

'I'm sure a CD would be better, but . . . with Hohozue's old audio system, I could only dub a cassette.'

Ken-chan shook his head lightly. 'No, a tape is actually better – the player Grandpa has is really old and can only do tapes.'

Ken-chan opened the case, and a little folded note peeked out. I'd copied out the lyric card that came with the album for him.

'Did you write all of this, Ryoko-chan? These lyrics are all in English . . .'

Ken-chan put the case in his pocket and unfolded the piece of paper. It was my favourite of all my stationery; I'd always felt like it would be a waste to use it, so I never had, but for this, I decided to open the pack.

For the pen, I tried using a blue ballpoint one made in France that a regular of the cafe who runs a trading company had given me. It had a different feel to it, and on top of that, I was writing unfamiliar English, so it had been pretty difficult.

I had the feeling that even my clumsy English letters looked fancy in navy ink on the mildly cream-coloured paper.

'Yeah – I mean, all I did was copy them. But there might be mistakes – because we haven't studied English yet. So I'll be really upset if you get mad at me for any mistakes.' I made a pouty face, and Ken-chan laughed.

'Thanks. I'll treasure it.'

'No, thank you! I'll take good care of this.'

I'd noticed that my dad was popping in and out of the kitchen to look at us. I wish he had left us alone for a little longer.

'Well, you better head back.'

'Yeah.' Ken-chan nodded as he put the lyric sheet back into the cassette case. 'Really, though, thanks. I've never had anything special happen on Christmas before. I always wondered what was so great about it. But now I feel like I understand – not completely, but a little better. I'm sure that's thanks to you. I appreciate it.' Ken-chan straightened up and bowed to me.

'Nooo, that's so overkill. OK, be careful on your way home.'

I gave his back a gentle push and followed him outside.

'Whoa, the snow piled up this much in such a short time . . .!'

The whole area was coated in white, and here and there, pristine footprints from passers-by remained. A delivery van happened to drive by just then, and two tyre tracks appeared on the road.

'Careful not to slip. If you fall, the cake'll be a mess.'

Bookmark

'Yeah, I'll be careful. You know when it's snowy, it's better not to step on the white lines or manhole covers. Those are more slippery than the tarmac.'

Are you really delivering this lecture now? I wanted to tease, but I didn't.

'Well, good night.' Ken-chan put his umbrella up.

'Not "good night" – Merry Christmas! We only get to say it one day a year!'

He chuckled and said, 'You know your stuff, huh? Then, "Merry Christmas".'

'Merry Christmas.'

I watched his back recede until he went out of sight.

'Ryoko. Hey, Ryoko!'

My eyes popped open at the sound of Ken-chan's voice. I must have fallen asleep at some point.

'Where are we?'

He said the name of the terminal station.

'Huh? When did that happen?'

'We just arrived.'

'Urgh, sorry. I fell asleep.'

I tried to get up in a rush.

'You don't have to hurry.'

Ken-chan took my Boston bag off the overhead rack and put it on his seat. I checked my book to make sure the bookmark was in it before putting it in the bag.

When I got up, Ken-chan held my coat open for me. He had been shorter than me for so long, but he shot past me in our second year of middle school, and now he stands about a head taller than me.

Notes from the Ginza Shihodo Stationery Shop

I said thanks and obediently put my arms through the sleeves. When someone who doesn't know what they're doing helps you with your coat, it can come off as pretentious, but perhaps because Ken-chan worked at a venerable old hotel between graduating university and returning to Shihodo, he pulled it off.

'In any case, we're pretty lucky. We may be two hours late, but we made it. The train after us got stopped at a mountain pass and can't go anywhere till morning. And the train after that got cancelled! We were right to leave when we did.'

'Hmm, I see . . .' I gave a disinterested response as I bundled up in my scarf. The city out the window was pure white; this was definitely record-breaking snowfall for Tokyo.

Ken-chan followed my gaze out the window and murmured, 'When we get back, I need to shovel at least the entrance and pavement. If it keeps snowing like this all night, it'll be a lot to handle in the morning.'

'Couldn't someone just make a rule already that when it snows eeeverything closes?' I grumbled with a huge sigh, and Ken-chan laughed.

'It's not as if we're King Hamehameha's kids.'

Our last train of our transfer for the night had already left, so, with no other choice, we headed for the taxi stand. Perhaps because the buses to more distant destinations were still running, the queue for taxis was short, and we were able to board after about five minutes.

After we piled into the back seat, Ken-chan gave the address. The driver seemed to be a veteran, and his head and full beard were all white. He was wearing a dark red jumper, so he looked just like Santa Claus.

Bookmark

'Your seatbelts are on, yes? Then we'll be on our way.'

Maybe he had tyre chains on? The ride felt different from usual, but he was a careful driver, and it felt almost like riding a sleigh over a field of snow.

The Imperial Palace's stone moat wall was powdered with snow, and even the buildings in the distance had an entirely different vibe from usual; it felt less like returning to Tokyo than like arriving in some unfamiliar town.

As I was steeping in the romance of that feeling, Ken-chan began rummaging around in the bag on his lap. I figured he was looking for gum or some sweets and nearly said, 'Stop wrecking the mood!' until he suddenly handed me something.

'Here you go. Really, I was planning to give it to you after we ate dinner.'

'Huh?'

When I turned on the car's lamp, I saw it was a long, slender box tied with a ribbon.

'It's a little early, but it's a Christmas present.'

When I undid the ribbon and opened the box, I found the fountain pen I'd been wanting inside: Pelikan's Souverän M400. The clip had a golden inscription that said *K to R*.

And with the fountain pen was a little card folded in half. The paper was a mild colour like an eggshell and had a rough feel to it. Yes, just like the bookmark. I was sure Ken-chan had made it himself.

Thanks for everything.
Looking forward to more time with you.
Ken

*

Notes from the Ginza Shihodo Stationery Shop

It was clearly Ken-chan's handwriting. As I looked, the characters began to blur.

I thought I should try to say something, but I couldn't for the life of me find the words. 'Thank you' was all I managed.

We happened to stop at a red light just then, and the car fell silent.

'You're welcome.'

With the sound of his voice in my ears, I dabbed at my eyes with a handkerchief.

'... You're awful, springing this on me like that.'

'Oh? Then I'll count the surprise as a grand success,' he said, cracking a smile, and I elbowed him.

'Honestly, just ... just ... thank you.'

'You're welcome.'

As if responding to Ken's reply, the light turned green.

Beyond the snow gliding across the windshield, Shihodo came into view.

* * *

'Package for you! I'll leave it with the rest of your post.'

The worker left the post on the edge of the desk and was off again right away. The innkeeper, who had been checking some numbers on the computer screen, removed her reading glasses and emitted a sigh.

'What are you sighing about?' her husband asked, taking his well-starched, white *waboshi* off his head. He had come in just as the worker was leaving.

'What am I sighing about? Ever since I married you it's been a parade of things that make me want to sigh ... By now, it's just habit. Of course, that wouldn't be acceptable in front of guests . . . Please at least let me do as I like in the office.'

'Sure, fine.' As if realising he should have left well alone, he escaped to the couch in the back of the room.

'Sheesh,' the innkeeper murmured as she picked up the little package that had arrived. On the invoice, the sender's name was listed as Ryoko Hayashida.

Inside were cookies and a letter.

My name is Hayashida – I visited the other day. You took very good care of us. Though the blizzard was unexpected, I'm very sorry that we cancelled at the last minute, and after soaking in the hot spring.

Despite that, you were so kind, not only arranging our tickets, but even giving us a ride to the station. Thank you so much. Plus the delicious bento you prepared for us? I don't know how to thank you enough.

We managed to make it back to Tokyo safely. Along the way, the snow grew heavy, and at times we worried what might happen, but thanks to the bento you prepared, we were able to wait it out calmly. I truly appreciate how meticulously thoughtful you were.

The person who came with me is someone I've known for ages, and we've always been mysteriously close – like friends, or cousins. This was our first longer-distance excursion together, so when the bad weather hit, I was upset and felt like luck just wasn't on my side, but in the end, I think it was a good trip.

I plan to keep working on our relationship, growing closer but never rushing.

Next time, I really want us to be able to enjoy 'Japan's

Notes from the Ginza Shihodo Stationery Shop

best breakfast'. Hope to see you then. I realise I should come by in person, but please allow me to express my gratitude with this letter.

Sincerely,
Ryoko Hayashida

PS I baked these at home. I'd be happy if you would accept them.

The paper and envelope were both quality washi that said Shihodo in the lower left corner. The characters, written with a fountain pen, were all neat, and the ink used was a beautiful blue with a sense of depth.

'Hey, I think it's about time for a snack. Is coffee OK for you?' The innkeeper hovered over her seat and called to the couch in the back.

'Anything's fine.'

'Could you please think for yourself and make a request once in a while? But today we've been given cookies, so coffee it is.'

The innkeeper switched the electric kettle on and began preparing the coffee.

'Hey, do you remember the day of the big snowstorm? Remember that couple who rushed back to Tokyo?'

'Ohhh, yeah, I remember them,' her husband responded without looking up from the newspaper.

'The woman sent cookies and a letter.'

When she held out the letter and cookies, her husband folded up the newspaper and took them.

'Wow, for being so young, she really has her act together.'

He slipped the letter out of the envelope and skimmed it before inspecting the box of cookies.

'These cookies were made with a lot of care, but I've never heard of Hohozue before.' He had the cafe's card in his hand. 'Sounds like it's in Ginza.'

'Oh? They look good, though, huh?'

'Yeah, let's see.' He grabbed a round one. 'Uh-huh. Yum. This flavour makes me kind of nostalgic. How to describe it? I guess it's a simple flavour made with just cake flour, sugar, eggs and butter? But they made sure to choose good quality.'

'Good quality . . . You know, the name of the person who sent this has the kanji for "good" in her name.'

'Oh, huh. Well, I'm sure it's just a coincidence . . .'

Vaguely annoyed by her husband's carefree response, the innkeeper shook her head. 'I do think "good child" is the perfect name for her. Her friend seemed a bit dense, though . . . Like someone else I know.'

'Hm? Did you say something?'

'No, nothing. Here's your coffee.'

The innkeeper set the cup before her husband and put the letter he had left out back in the envelope. Then she murmured to the name of the sender written on it: 'Hang in there!'

Coloured Pencils

'I read the script and prepared several design options.'

As I was pulling up the rough drafts on my tablet, the interpreter spoke Japanese. Apparently the director was quite major in Japan, and the interpreter chose awfully polite language. *I wasn't being* that *modest*, I thought, but I bit my tongue.

The director took the tablet I held out and began looking over the designs.

He didn't say a word about what he thought, just scrolled silently through.

The project was a stage version of an anime that had become a hit around the world. Not a single cast member had been announced yet, but people were already paying attention. I'm one of the founders of a studio that specialises in theatre sets and props, and I'd been selected as the scenic designer for the show. The purpose of my trip to Japan this time was to talk to the director about how we'd proceed together and what direction we wanted to go in.

'Hmm . . .' After checking all the designs, he glanced at me and said, 'They're not bad.'

The interpreter immediately said, 'I think they're good,' in English.

'I'm pretty sure "not bad" doesn't mean "good",' I shot back in Japanese before I even realised.

'. . . You know Japanese?' the director said stiffly.

To the panicking interpreter, I said, 'Sorry, I don't mean to be rude, but please let me speak to him directly,' and then continued. 'My mother is Japanese, and I lived in Japan through elementary school.'

'... I see.'

'For more involved discussions or contract details, there might be barriers, of course, but for matters of taste, I'll be OK. Please give me your honest impressions.'

He stared at me for a moment and then nodded firmly. 'OK. That's better for me, too. I'm not a fan of convoluted communications. "Not bad" means just that – "not bad". That is, not bad enough to disparage it by saying it's poorly done or worthless. Just ... how to say ...'

'There's nothing surprising about it? It's not interesting?'

'Huh ...' the director murmured. 'If you understand that much, then I'd like to see you put a little more effort in.'

I sat up straighter and flipped open my notepad. 'Understood. May I ask something?'

'Go ahead.'

I heard the Japanese staff members hold their breath. Maybe in their world questioning this director wasn't allowed.

'How faithful to the anime do you want to be?'

The director was the executive director who had written the script and designed the characters for the anime, so in the studio we'd been debating how far we could stray from his unique vision.

'You don't have to worry about it at all. I'd like you to create something based solely on the script and the project outline. I can't see any point in doing the same thing on the stage as we did with the anime. Even if the fundamental theme is the same,

Coloured Pencils

I believe that anime and theatre have distinct modes of expression that should be utilised to the fullest.'

The staff members began to murmur to each other.

'Understood. I'll rethink it.'

He nodded deeply at my reply and then continued. 'Just one thing. I want you to pay attention to colour. I want a richer palette than the type of ordinary colours you could pick out by number from a chart. Like, imagine you're literally adding splashes of colour to the story.'

'That's a tall order.'

'You've won enough Tonys that it should be a cinch for you, no, Davis-san?'

I shook my head. 'Set and props come together through the work of a great number of people. It requires not only staff at my studio, but the cooperation of external workshops and design companies. The more people involved, the more precise the numerical values have to be in order to avoid errors.'

'That goes for anime production as well. I'm using the latest digital technology, so I understand the pitfalls of using vague language when syncing with staff members and tech experts. I'm not saying, "Don't use colour charts as a communication tool." Just that I want to avoid using the colours as the numbers indicate and putting them together like a puzzle.'

I didn't not understand what he was getting at.

'I'll remember that.'

He nodded deeply, seeming satisfied with my response. 'Let's meet again next week at the same time.'

His words were polite, but he was telling me to redo everything in a single week. I hadn't been treated like this in a long time. It was like going back to my days labouring in obscurity, and rather than feeling angry, I was compelled to action.

'I'll do my best.'

The director stood and offered his hand. 'I'm sure I won't be disappointed.' *The scene would've come off so much better if you had skipped the handshake and just given me a silent nod before walking away . . .* I thought as we shook.

When the director left, his large entourage went with him. Once it was just me and the interpreter, I bowed my head to her. 'I'm sorry I went ahead and did everything in Japanese.'

'No . . . I'm sorry. It's my fault for being a bad interpreter.'

I shook my head. 'No, I don't think that's the issue. I get the sense it's not your English ability but your feelings towards the director that are getting in the way. Am I wrong?'

'I've been following him ever since his debut. I've always wanted to collaborate and create something together. I worked my butt off and managed to get into his company, but I can't draw and I'm not good at coming up with stories. I volunteered for this because I thought maybe if it were English, I could be of use to him as an interpreter, but I couldn't. We should have hired a specialist from outside the company after all.'

'If you care about him, please translate exactly what he says. Without fear. If you interpret too freely based on what you imagine his feelings are, it can cause misunderstandings.'

She nodded firmly.

'So please come to the meeting next week and help us both out. I'll be counting on you.'

'Are you sure you want me?'

'I need your help. Sure, I speak a little Japanese, but it's been decades since I last set foot on Japanese soil, and there are so

Coloured Pencils

many things I don't know. So please be my lifeline. I'm sure helping me means helping him, too.'

'OK...'

'Oh, you can help me right now...' I took a product out of my bag. 'Do you know where the shop on this sticker is?'

The next day, I headed to the place the interpreter had marked on my map app.

'Apparently there's one of those cylindrical postboxes you don't see around much these days. And the old building facing it is Shihodo.'

There was indeed a vermilion postbox standing there as if it had got mixed in with the willow trees lining the street. Maybe the newer postboxes with squared corners are better functionally, but you'd be hard-pressed to find a more charming design. It seemed to be made of cast iron, and maybe because it was getting regular paint jobs to prevent rust, the vermilion was positively dazzling.

'Hey, how ya doin'?' I felt like I'd run into an old friend, and I petted the postbox's head. At the rough feel of the texture, I suddenly had the feeling I'd been here before.

I turned around to find a short flight of stone steps leading to a pair of glass doors. The doors were polished to the point you could mistake them for a mirror, and each had gold characters that said *Shihodo* in the centre. I took a small, deep breath before walking up the steps and pushing the doors open.

Entering the shop, I was met with cool air. Though summer wasn't yet in full force, I was sweaty after a short walk, so it felt good. And it wasn't as if the air conditioner was blasting, either. It was the pleasant feel of a breeze blowing over clear running

Notes from the Ginza Shihodo Stationery Shop

water. When I looked up at the ceiling, I saw that a fan with large blades was slowly turning.

Upon taking a few steps, I was enveloped in a fragrance like cedarwood. No, maybe it was incense? Some scent that made me feel nostalgic.

The exterior was dignified stone, but inside, what left an impression were the pure white, perhaps plaster walls; sunlight streamed through the large windows facing the street, creating a bright, airy atmosphere. The floor seemed to have been carefully waxed and polished – it had the dull gleam of a Noh stage. On the display shelves made primarily of wood, all different kinds of writing materials asserted themselves while still maintaining the balance of the space, which is much harder to arrange than it looks.

'Welcome. Thank you for coming. May I help you?' The staff member who appeared from the back must have thought I was a foreign tourist – he spoke English.

'Yes, I'm looking for coloured pencils.' I took a case of coloured pencils out of my bag.

'Oh, Mitsubishi. Those are pretty old, huh?' he said to himself in Japanese, perhaps without thinking.

'Yes, I've been using them since I was a kid.' The moment I said it, I thought, *Damn . . .* A friend had told me before I left the US that I should be careful not to respond to a Japanese person speaking English with Japanese because it would really hurt their self-esteem.

But the man from the shop didn't seem upset. He just smiled a bit bashfully and bowed his head before saying in Japanese, 'Apologies for addressing you in my poor English. Please forgive me.'

Coloured Pencils

That was a bit of a shock. 'No, there was nothing wrong with it at all. Your pronunciation was very fluent. Have you lived abroad?'

'Never! I just worked at a hotel briefly a long time ago ... And given the location of the shop, we do get customers from overseas, so I can really only muddle through some customer service. If you don't mind, could we continue in Japanese?'

He seemed quite young, though he must have been in his late thirties. His politeness and humble attitude reminded me of the person I recalled being here.

'Of course. Actually, my mother is Japanese. And I lived in Japan through elementary school, so I learned Japanese first. That said, we moved to the States just before I started middle school, and I haven't been back in all those decades. So I might sometimes sound a little weird or out of date.'

The man took a business card out of his pocket. 'Ken Takarada, the manager of Shihodo Stationery, at your service.'

That surprised me. I figured he was just on staff, but he was running the place. I rushed to get a card out of my jacket pocket.

'I'm Tommy Davis. I do set design and stuff for plays and musicals.'

He looked between my face and the card for a moment before emitting a little yelp. 'Tommy Davis-san who was creative director of the Broadway musical *Circus*?! I, uh, I saw it ... last year!'

Apparently he had seen one of the performances in Japan the previous year. Unfortunately, I was busy with another show and couldn't be there, but I'm pretty sure the pamphlet they sold at the theatre featured my headshot and profile.

'Oh, you did?'

'Yes, I thought the musical itself was wonderful, but that set really impressed me. The way it changed completely depending on the lighting – it could appear both showy and shabby even though there weren't any major set changes. It was so unexpected.'

I couldn't help but crack a smile. 'I'm thrilled it stuck in the mind of someone who saw it. But I guess I need to take a lesson from it, too. The set, costumes and so on are only there to highlight the story. They should never outshine the actors.'

Ken responded, 'That's tricky . . .' before continuing, 'but I do think the symbol that united all those actors of different backgrounds from various countries and regions was the big-top set.' Having said that much, he suddenly emitted an, 'Ah!' and scratched the back of his head self-consciously. '. . . Excuse me. I got a little overexcited. I hope you'll forgive me.'

'Not at all. It's not every day that I get to hear directly from someone who's seen one of my shows. But you're a rare type. I think there are a lot of people who remember the names of actors and directors, or playwrights, but not many who pay attention to people working on the set.'

Takarada-san nodded, looking a bit embarrassed. 'I'm interested in spatial direction. Originally, my goal was to improve the displays at the shop, so I went around to see how it was done at department stores and boutiques, but somewhere along the line my interest expanded to displays in larger spaces, such as train stations, museums, airports and so on. Then, when a long-time acquaintance invited me to see a play, I became fascinated by scenic design . . .'

Somehow I felt I had learned the secret behind the shop's meticulously calculated interior. As I had guessed, it was a reflection of the owner's character.

Coloured Pencils

'Now then, you're a customer, so setting aside my curiosity as a fan, I'd like to hear what I can help you with, Davis-sama,' Takarada-san said, straightening up. The childlike innocence of a moment ago vanished, and he put on his stationery shop manager 'hat'.

'Do you have this same set? I have a few colours that have got awfully short, so I'd like to buy some new ones.'

'Coloured pencils, I see.'

Upon accepting the box I held out reverently with both hands, he said, 'Right this way,' and guided me to a section further inside. 'Here are the coloured pencils. Your average stationery shop will carry mainly sets, but we have a wide selection of loose pencils as well.'

The display was packed with all kinds of coloured pencils.

'What a sight!'

'Thank you. The set you have is quite old, so we may not have exactly the same ones, but I think this Colored Pencil No. 880 series will be a close match.'

The shelf he indicated had thirty-six colours. Next to it was another series with more than double the colours.

'That's also from the Mitsubishi Pencil Company – their Uni Colored Pencil series. They're higher grade than the 880s and come in 100 colours. Incidentally, we only sell them by the set, but we also have their Uni Water Color series of pencils, which allow artists to create the soft touch of watercolours by blending the pencil pigment with a wet paintbrush, as well as the Uni Arterase Color series, which are neatly erasable – rare for coloured pencils.'

They all piqued my interest, and I wanted to try them.

'That's fantastic. Makes me want to test all sorts of things.

Notes from the Ginza Shihodo Stationery Shop

But first I'd like to buy replacements for my pencils that have gotten too short, please.'

With a respectful, 'Understood,' Takarada-san opened the tin case. In the corner, under the lid, was a little golden sticker. The print had faded, but it was still possible to read: *Engraving by Shihodo Stationery, Ginza*.

'Given the sticker, I would guess these were purchased here forty or fifty years ago?'

'Yes, my grandfather got them for me when I started elementary school, so I think it was over forty years ago.'

Takarada-san set the case on the edge of the display shelf and picked up the short colours. 'Red, yellow, green and blue – are those the ones you would like?'

'Yes, that's right. Oh, and would it be possible to get them engraved in the same way?'

He gave me a deep nod. 'Yes, of course; however . . . we began offering engravings as a perk for customers who purchased a set, so if you buy loose pencils, there's a service charge. Also, it takes a little time to do the work, so if you don't mind waiting . . .'

He looked apologetic. It takes effort, so it shouldn't be an issue to confidently charge a fee and require some time, but maybe that didn't fly in Japan? No, that didn't seem right. It must have been the proud nature of a venerable Ginza establishment that has been in business for so long.

'Of course. I'm planning to stay in Japan for a couple weeks. Is that enough time?'

'Yes, the engraving itself doesn't take very long . . . I just run the shop by myself, so there isn't much time during the day I can settle into the task. I'll do it after we close today, so they'll be ready for you tomorrow or any day after that.'

Coloured Pencils

'You're going to do it tonight?' I asked before I could stop myself.

'Yes, I do my best to fulfil orders as soon as I get them.'

'Then, would it be possible for me to observe? I like watching handiwork in progress – seeing what kinds of tools or machines are involved, what order the steps happen in and so on. If you don't mind, I'll come back after closing time. What do you think?'

Takarada-san's face was hesitant for a moment, but after thinking it over, he nodded.

'If you're all right coming back, that's fine, but it's not very exciting work, so I'm afraid you might be underwhelmed.'

'No worries.'

'All right. Oh, and you'd like the same gold hiragana?' said Takarada-san as he picked up the longest pencil – purple.

'Yes, *Tomio Sahara*. That's my Japanese name.'

Just as Takarada-san said, 'Understood,' there came the sound of the door opening. When I turned around, I saw a beautiful woman in a perfectly white blouse with a bow tie and pencil skirt.

As I gazed in fascination, she approached and said, 'Irasshaimase,' with a bow. She was carrying a wicker basket.

'You're welcoming me?' I was confused.

'Oh, excuse me. I ordered coffee from a cafe in the neighbourhood. Ryoko, this is Davis-san. Do you remember going to see that musical, *Circus*, last year? He's the one who designed the set.'

Ryoko-san beamed and said, 'What! Really? Nice to meet you. My name is Ryoko Hayashida.'

'Tommy Davis. You're gorgeous. Are you Takarada-san's girlfriend?'

'Oh, no, she's an old friend . . . practically family.'

I could tell there were subtleties to the relationship from the way he said 'family'.

'I see . . .'

When I nodded deeply, Ryoko-san hung her head in embarrassment.

'Oh, right. This is good timing. Hey, Ryoko, could you watch the shop for a bit? I'd like to do the coloured pencil engraving he ordered.'

'Sure. The cafe's been slow today anyhow.' Ryoko-san gave a willing reply.

'Oh no, I wouldn't want to put you out like that . . . No need to bend over backwards. I'll come again this evening.'

When I demurred, Ryoko-san responded with a beautiful smile.

'Think nothing of it. It'll be an excuse for me to take a break, too.'

Takarada-san nodded in agreement and said, 'All right, then, let me show you the way. The workshop is in the basement. Oh, I'll take that.' He grabbed the basket from Ryoko-san and beckoned to me with his other hand.

I followed him, and we came to an ascending staircase at the end of the aisle. Next to it was an inconspicuous door that almost looked like part of the wall at first glance. When Takarada-san pushed the handle with a finger, the door noiselessly opened.

Perhaps there was a sensor? Footlights automatically illuminated the stairs. When I went through the door, it silently closed behind me. Had it been built on a slight slope? Or were there weights or springs involved?

When we reached the basement, Takarada-san turned the

lights on. Perhaps because it was a workshop, bright LED lights lit the room. A few machines that appeared to be printing presses were there. Next to that was a worktable, a rack filled with type and shelves filled with some sort of inventory or other.

'Ooh . . .' I couldn't help but sigh in admiration.

'All the machines are old . . . All the manufacturers have gone out of business, so there's no surefire way to get them repaired and maintained.'

My eyes stopped on a machine in the corner. It was a small handpress, which could be used to print smaller items such as postcards or business cards.

'This is a *tekin*, right?'

'Right, you know your stuff. I started printing business cards again recently using this machine.'

'Is it possible to make orders in English?' I asked before thinking. Ordering business cards on a vintage letterpress in the US would cost a pretty penny.

'Of course, but printing a logo or other special symbols requires some time and an extra fee. It would start from commissioning a mould, and only a limited number of places are creating new moulds and type these days. You would have to be prepared to wait.'

'I see . . .'

As he politely answered my question, he folded the cloth that had been covering the worktable. Beneath it was something like a laminator.

'Is this what you use for engraving?'

'Yes. Actually, the newer machine next to it can do a dozen at a time and doesn't require type or a mould, so if there's no special instructions, I use that. Your pencils, though, must have been done with the old machine, so I thought it would be best if they matched.'

Takarada-san pulled two nearby chairs over to the worktable and offered one to me before excusing himself and also taking a seat. Then he powered up the machine and began fishing type out of a box.

'I don't want to bother you while you work, but do you mind if I ask a question?'

He glanced at me and then nodded. 'Yes, of course. I'm used to the work, so actually it'll go faster if you talk to me.'

'Oh, good . . . then I won't hold back. I'm curious about pencil shapes. Why are regular pencil shafts often hexagonal while coloured pencil shafts are always round? Of course, some regular pencils are round – like the ones sold as character merch, but I think pretty much all coloured pencils are.'

Takarada-san nodded as he lined up the six characters in a slim, rectangular frame. 'The reason usually given for hexagonal pencils is that they're easier to hold. The grip generally considered suitable for writing involves holding the shaft with the thumb, index finger and middle finger. In other words, you hold three sides, so a shaft with a number of sides that is a multiple of three will be easier to hold. But a triangular shape would mean pointy sixty-degree angles, which would make your fingers sore after a while. Nine or twelve sides would take longer to make and push manufacturing prices up. That's how we ended up with six-sided pencils. In contrast, coloured pencils are used for drawing and might be held in a number of different ways, so it's said that they're kept round to accommodate any hand position. There are different theories and opinions, so I'm not really sure what's true, but . . .'

Coloured Pencils

'I see, so it's based on ergonomics,' I murmured with a deep nod, and Takarada-san continued.

'It's also said that the lead comes into it.'

'The lead?'

'Yes, pencil lead is a mixture of graphite and clay that is stirred and formed before firing. The firing process makes it more durable – less likely to break, but it would affect the colours of the coloured pencils, so clay is not used, nor is the lead fired. Coloured pencil lead is pigment mixed with an adhesive like talcum powder, paste or wax to harden it. For that reason, the lead breaks more easily than regular pencil lead.'

'Ahhh . . .'

'So regular pencil lead and coloured pencil lead have different thicknesses.' Takarada-san took one of the coloured pencils we'd brought from the sales floor and a regular pencil from the desk and held them with the ends lined up so it would be easy to see the lead. 'A normal pencil's lead is usually about 2 millimetres in diameter. A coloured pencil's is usually 3 to 3.5.'

It was only about a millimetre's difference, but even at a glance, it was clear one was thicker than the other.

'So it's also said that the round shape was chosen to encase the more easily breakable lead with a uniform thickness of coating.'

'I see. I never even realised the lead was different thicknesses,' I murmured without really meaning to.

'Well, these days, it seems the tech has improved, so the lead is less fragile than it used to be. At this point, it might be the case that coloured pencils are made round out of habit.'

As Takarada-san spoke, he finished setting up the machine. Then, I suppose to confirm the positioning, he took the purple pencil out of the case and glanced between it and the frame.

'OK, we're good to go,' he said softly.

Then he took the blue pencil from the sales floor and set it in the machine. After checking the position of the gold sheet, he used his right hand to push the lever down.

'How does this look?' Takarada-san held out the blue pencil, along with the original purple one for comparison. The purple pencil had some knicks and scratches, and the gold engraved letters were somewhat faded, but both engravings were in exactly the same typeface and position.

'... Looks good.'

Takarada-san smiled in relief and did the remaining three pencils.

'That's it for the engraving, but shall I sharpen them so you can use them right away?'

'Oh, please do.'

Takarada-san nodded and took a small tool out from a drawer in the worktable. A clear plastic cylinder was capped with what seemed like machined aluminium. In the top was a hole about the size of a pencil equipped with a dully gleaming steel blade.

When he inserted the red-coloured pencil and twisted, a carnation bloomed inside the plastic cylinder with a pleasant shaving sound. No, it was just the pencil shavings, but they were practically a work of art, they were so beautiful.

Perhaps noticing my eyes were riveted on the tool, Takarada-san put the finished red pencil on the worktable and offered me the sharpener.

'It's OK for me to use it?'

'Certainly. This is made by Nakajima Jukyudo, a company that specialises in pencil sharpeners. They have original brands, but also act as an OEM for overseas writing utensil companies. If you like it, we have the model in stock here. Please give it a try.'

I took the sharpener from him, put a pencil in and twisted. The blade inside must have had quite a good edge on it – a light touch was enough to start shaving the tip into a neat cone. The shavings weren't shredded; instead, they came off like an endless spiral staircase.

Enjoying the pleasant sensations on the palm of my hand, I finished sharpening the rest of the pencils.

'If you need to do a lot of pencils at once, an electric sharpener or one with a crank is convenient, but the strong vibrations do put a lot of pressure on the pencil. Coloured pencils especially need to be handled with care because their lead is more fragile, as I explained earlier. So I would recommend a manual sharpener.'

'Yes, this is wonderful. I'd definitely like to buy one.'

'Great, we can do that later. There's also a smaller version for carrying around, so you can choose according to how you think you'll use it,' said Takarada-san as he took the three pencils I'd sharpened. 'By the way, what will you do with the pencils that are too short? Do you want to take them home? Otherwise I could hold on to them here and take them to a *fude kuyo* service.'

'Fude kuyo?'

Takarada-san nodded gently. 'Yes, they hold them at certain shrines, like Tenmangu, which all enshrine Sugawara no Michizane – the god of academics who is also said to be the god of calligraphy. The memorials were originally for brushes that have reached the end of their usefulness, but these days they also accept pencils, fountain pens and so on.'

'I see . . . How very Japanese.'

I took the four pencil stubs out of the case. I had used them with care, but there wasn't much I could do with them now that they were this short. Still, I couldn't bear to throw them in the bin.

I presented them to Takarada-san using both hands. 'Please take them to a memorial for me. I appreciate it.'

He said, 'Understood,' and bowed his head as he accepted my stubby pencils. Then he took a tin about the size of a tissue box off a shelf near the worktable, opened the lid and gently set them inside. I caught a glimpse of the contents: worn-down pencils, calligraphy brushes, fountain pens and more. On the outside, there was a paper label – perhaps written with a calligraphy brush? – that said *For Fude Kuyo* in bold characters.

Takarada-san put the new pencils in the gaps left by the short ones he'd taken. Then he confirmed the condition of each of the old pencils one by one, taking them out and then arranging them so the colour names were visible and sharpening the tips of those that had gone round. The motions of his hands were so full of care, like a barber making final trims.

'Oh?' Takarada-san's hands suddenly stopped. 'What's this?'

I cracked a smile. 'So you noticed.'

He picked up the so-called 'tea-coloured' – brown – pencil. Then the peach, then the light blue. The parts where the colour names were engraved were slightly darker, and the names had been changed.

'Did . . . Shihodo do this alteration?'

I nodded slowly and pointed at the case. 'Even the inside of the case. Take a closer look.'

'Oh, you're right . . .'

The original characters had been painted over with a steely grey and characters in the same style had been written over

Coloured Pencils

the top. Right after it was done, it stood out, but after all these decades, it had blended in to the point that you had to really look to notice.

Takarada-san examined the lid and pencils and emitted a little sigh. 'The work does look like my grandfather's . . . People think I get overly involved in other people's business, but clearly I'm nothing compared to him. If you don't mind, I'd love to hear the story.'

His tone had changed subtly from his courteous shop manager manner.

'Yes, of course. Is your grandfather . . . ?'

Takarada-san shook his head slightly. 'He joined the dead a few years ago.'

'I see . . . I wish I had come sooner.' I heaved a sigh.

When Takarada-san saw that, he replied warmly, 'I'm sure just the fact that you came makes him happy.'

Then he opened the basket he'd brought down and poured iced coffee out of the thermos inside.

'It's refreshing yet has good depth of flavour, so I recommend drinking it black. They deliver it well-chilled from being in the fridge, so I don't add ice.'

I obediently took a sip of it as it was offered. It was true that the flavour was very clean, and it went down easy. Yet its fragrance also asserted itself, flowing through my nasal passages.

'All right, then let's take a little trip down memory lane.'

Having wet my whistle, I lightly crossed my legs.

I was born in Japan around the time Nixon became President of the United States. My father was an officer in the American army, and he was stationed in Japan as rear support for the

Notes from the Ginza Shihodo Stationery Shop

Vietnam War. He was already married and had a family in the States, but he fell in love with my mother, who was working with him as an interpreter, and they had me.

A few months later when his assignment in Japan was finished, he told my mother, 'I'll be back for you, so please wait for me,' and went back to the US. My mother took me, still an infant, and went to live with my grandfather, who was on his own.

He'd lost his wife too soon and raised his daughter as a single father. How must he have felt when that daughter showed up with a baby she'd had with an American? I'm sure he felt conflicted. I didn't find out until much later, but he had been drafted and sent into battle. Not only that, but he was one of the few who miraculously survived an area of extremely heavy fighting at the end of the war and had experienced the kind of combat that was so close and intense he could feel his enemies breathing.

During the time my mother and I stayed with him, he was running a patent attorney office, making his living handling patents, utility models and the like for clients such as nearby factories. The little house he'd acquired before the war just barely escaped being burned, so he didn't have any issue with a place to live, but I'm sure he wasn't so well off that he could provide for us.

When I turned three, my mother left me with my grandfather, who worked from home, and went out to work. Having been saddled with me, he probably didn't have much choice, but he really did look after me, and I'm thankful for that.

That said, it wasn't as if he doted on me. He'd hand me a botched document-turned-scrap paper, give me a pencil and say, 'Go and draw a picture or something.' When I drew something, he'd be impressed and say, 'Oh, Tomio, you're quite the artist,'

Coloured Pencils

praising me often. I was delighted to get his praise, so I drew picture after picture. It was around that age that I fell in love with drawing, but I'm sure it was because getting complimented so much made me happy.

My father had promised to return for us, but that day never quite came. Before I knew it, I was in elementary school.

When I started school, my grandfather got me a randoseru, pencil case and so on. One of the supplies he prepared was a set of twenty-four coloured pencils. Until that time, I'd been drawing with a graphite pencil that had got too short for my grandfather to use, so I'd never added colour before.

'I can use these?'

He nodded emphatically. 'Of course. I got them for you, Tomio. I went to a venerable old stationery shop in Ginza, the best town in Japan, and had them put your name on each one.'

He held out the red pencil and I saw that it had *Tomio Sahara* engraved in gleaming golden characters. I couldn't read the characters, but I understood that it was my name, and even as a kid I understood well that I'd received a gift of fine quality.

'And that was this set?'

I nodded softly.

Takarada-san picked up the half-gone green and the red he'd just engraved from the case sitting between us. 'My predecessor was skilled at this kind of work. He left behind some samples, but I can't seem to match them. Hexagonal shafts are relatively easy since they have flat faces, but round shafts have to be impressed on a curved surface, so it's difficult to gauge how much pressure to use. If you press too hard, the centre will be ruined, but if you don't press hard enough, the outer edges won't show up. If he were to appraise my work today, I'd be lucky if he said, "Well, it's a pass, but just barely."'

I couldn't tell any difference between the two engravings.

'Fifty years ago or so, getting pencils engraved seemed to be the thing to do. Did friends have similar sets?'

I thought for a moment. 'I'm sure you're right, Takarada-san, but I wouldn't know, because while classmates become classmates automatically, I don't think I ever made a single friend.'

Takarada-san's face fell.

'Because I look like a foreigner. And regardless of what it's like now, in Japan fifty years ago, it was the Showa period.'

For kindergarten I went to a place run by a church that my grandfather found a bit of a way away. There was a British teacher there and some international kids, so I wasn't seen as something out of the ordinary all that often. Or maybe I was so small my appearance wasn't as obvious yet.

As graduation from kindergarten and the start of elementary school grew near, there were some times my mother and grandfather argued late at night. I heard from my mother much later that he wanted to put me in an international school, like the kindergarten I'd been going to, or a private school with an emphasis on international education.

But my mother still believed my father was coming back. 'As soon as he comes, we'll be off to the US. We have no idea when it might be, so we can't go spending so much money on expensive tuition,' she'd said, refusing to listen. That was how I ended up enrolled at the local public elementary school.

The nickname they gave me there was Sambo.

*

Coloured Pencils

'Sambo?' Takarada-san's voice cracked.

'Yes, have you heard of it? Every library used to have a copy of the picture book . . .' I took out my phone and showed him the cover: red with a Black boy in the centre holding a green umbrella, surrounded by four tigers.

'Ohhh, this? I'm pretty sure it was put out of print because it perpetuated racism, right? But I heard another publisher picked it up . . .' Takarada-san told me as he looked at my phone.

'Ahh, I see . . . I thought there were some interesting parts, like the tigers running around the tree and melting into butter, and the part where the family eats the pancakes. But now I can be honest and say that, at the time, I really hated that book.'

Takarada-san sighed. 'It must have been unbearable . . .'

'It was a long time ago.'

'Hey, Sambo, did you have pancakes for breakfast today?'

One of the notorious bullies in the neighbourhood teased me practically every day. It got especially bad once we ended up in the same class in fourth grade.

'Sambo, what's with the curled-up hair? Did you get a perm or something?'

'You're lookin' awfully tan. Should I lather you up with tanning oil?'

He'd bring his three friends and run circles around me, calling me names, kicking my randoseru, pulling on my lunch bag, and the bullying would last all the way to school. I used to think, *I wish you'd run faster and melt into butter!* But nothing changed.

From about that time, I started to grow a lot, and I got standout values in the strength tests we did at school, too. I think

Notes from the Ginza Shihodo Stationery Shop

I could have held my own against the bullies in a fight, but I detested violence. No matter what happened, I endured it and went home to cry alone. There were a number of times I thought to ask my mother and grandfather for help, but I knew if I said something, they would worry, so I couldn't bring myself to consult them. I just sniffled on my own, drawing manga characters or something to distract myself.

At times like that, my grandfather would bring me a cup of tea or cocoa but leave me be, saying only, 'Be careful, it's hot.' Before he left my room, my mouth would nearly open more than once, but in the end, I said nothing.

So that was how fourth grade was going; then, there was an incident. It happened while we were on a field trip to a factory. After seeing how things worked, we were borrowing a meeting room to fill out our 'Field Report' sheets. There was a space on the sheet to draw a picture of us learning about the factory.

'Hey, Sambo. Make sure to colour your face in black!'

I was drawing carefully with my coloured pencils, using my art skills, when the bully came over to my seat. When I ignored him and continued drawing, he plucked one of my coloured pencils out of the case.

'You don't need this "skin colour" one, huh?' In the next moment, he'd dropped the pencil on the floor and was about to stomp on it.

'Don't!'

I jumped out of my chair, reached for the pencil and brushed his leg away. When he lost his balance, he must have fallen weird, because he burst into tears holding his arm.

That day, after everyone had gone home, I was stuck in the principal's office waiting for a guardian to pick me up. My

Coloured Pencils

mother was working or something and couldn't come right away, so my grandfather came.

The moment he walked into the room, he asked, 'Are you OK?' I nodded in silence and then the vice-principal spoke.

'It seems a lot has been going on between Tomio-kun and the child in question. And today he was teasing him about the colour of his skin and making comments about his coloured pencils . . . But Tomio-kun was the first one to get physical this time. Regardless of what was happening, laying a hand on someone and going so far as to injure them is . . . I'll tell you where he lives, so please take Tomio-kun and pay a visit to apologise.'

My grandfather didn't answer, but just peered into my face. 'Tomio, is that true?'

I shook my head and explained how the bully had taken one of my pencils and was about to stomp it, and that all I'd done was brush his leg away.

'So that's his story. I don't see how my grandson is at fault. I don't understand why he should have to apologise when he was only trying to get the kid to stop messing with him.'

'But . . .' The vice-principal exchanged bewildered glances with the principal and my teacher.

'Please tell the other kid and his parents that just because Tomio puts up with it doesn't mean he can do whatever he wants and get away with it. If they have a problem with that, they can come and see me. I won't run or hide.'

My grandfather was a calm man of few words; I'd never seen him speak so forcefully before.

On the way home, he didn't say a word to me. He just whistled softly, holding my hand tight. The fragmented, raspy sounds were also sometimes out of tune, so I couldn't tell what song it was.

That night, my mother came home late, so Grandpa made dinner for me. We had katsu, my favourite. Breading and frying the meat was a pain, so the dish didn't appear on our table except on special occasions – he must have been trying to cheer me up.

Making laps between the kitchen and our low table, he fed me freshly fried katsu. Once he'd finished cooking, relaxed into his seat and picked up his chopsticks, he pincered a piece of katsu, examined it thoughtfully, and murmured, 'We call the colour of nicely fried katsu *kitsuneiro*, right? I wonder why that is.'

The sudden question caught me off guard, and I laughed. 'Huh? How should I know?'

'Well, yeah . . .' He took a bite. 'Mm, good,' he said with a smile. 'It's not as if any fox is that colour. Oh, is it because it looks like the fried tofu that goes on kitsune udon?'

'Who knows?' I replied with little enthusiasm. Instead, I took my coloured pencils out of my school bag and drew katsu in my sketchbook. Using brown, yellow and red, adding accents and highlights as I went, I layered colours until I had a tasty-looking katsu.

'You really are a good artist.'

As usual, I was happy to be praised.

'I wonder if there's a kitsuneiro pencil.'

I swapped the pencil out for my chopsticks and finished eating my katsu.

'I wonder . . . But, you know, I think most colours are called what they are because those are the names they've had for a long time. Out of habit, so to speak. I'm sure "skin colour" is the same. So . . . so don't let all the stuff those dummies say bother you.'

Coloured Pencils

'You're normal, so it's easy for you to say,' I snapped back in spite of myself.

'Normal...? What does "normal" mean? Who decides that? I think it's just a word people use when they want to be evasive about something they don't understand very well...'

I felt like he was saying something complicated to gloss it over, which annoyed me. 'You should try standing in my shoes... If this is how it was gonna be, I wish I'd never been born.'

Grandpa set his chopsticks down, straightened up and looked me square in the eye.

'Maybe my last comment was hard to understand. Maybe I haven't managed to understand the struggles you're going through. If it wasn't up to scratch, I apologise. I'm sorry. But never say you wish you'd never been born. Please take that back – it's better for you that way, too.'

His voice was very hard. I didn't talk back, just started to cry. When I looked, I saw his cheeks were wet too.

'There might be hard times in life. But no matter how hard it gets, never say you wish you'd never been born. There are so many people who aren't able to survive even if they want to. We can't forget that.'

His voice was soft, but his words pierced my heart deeply.

'I'm sorry...'

'As long as you understand, it's all right.'

After that, we were both silent for a time. I wonder what he was thinking.

After a little while, he took a pencil out of the case lying open on the tatami.

'I realise I bought this set for you, but looking at them now, I see lots of colours have weird names...'

Hearing that, I wiped away my tears with the back of my hands and said, 'Yeah, I thought so too. Like, why *mizuiro*? Water doesn't even have a colour – it's clear.'

'Yeah. *Chairo* is also goofy, huh? Tea is yellow. And tea leaves are green!'

'I'd understand if it were *mugichairo*.' Barley tea is brown.

'Yes, that would make sense . . .' He examined each pencil, shaking his head. 'Well, I think every colour name is just a word that stuck when someone long ago said, "This'll be the name for this colour."'

'You think so . . .?'

In response to my doubtful expression, he said, 'OK, let's go out somewhere together tomorrow.'

'Huh? But I have school tomorrow . . .'

I was kind of shocked, but he shook his head. 'What kind of dummy would go to such an infuriating school as if it's *sooo* damned important? Take a day off!'

I was surprised to hear him curse.

'Really? Won't Mom get mad?'

'Don't worry, I'll convince her. Leave that to me.'

He thumped his chest theatrically and practically inhaled the rest of his katsu.

'What a wonderful person your grandfather was.' Takarada-san smiled gently. It was very similar to the smile I'd seen decades ago.

The next day, I left the house with my grandfather. As we were leaving, he somewhat aggressively told my mother, 'I'm giving Tomio the day off. You call the school and tell them he

Coloured Pencils

won't be there,' and then asked me, 'Do you have your coloured pencils?'

We transferred trains a few times before disembarking at a large station just before noon.

'Where are we?'

He gave the answer in a leisurely fashion. 'Ginza.'

After that, I'm sure we walked all around, but I don't really remember the details. What I do remember clearly is an incredibly detailed Z-scale diorama with a model steam engine running around the track, and that my grandfather got me Naporitan pasta and a melon soda float for lunch.

After lunch, he murmured to himself, 'OK, now should be a good time.'

'Time for what?'

'Hm? Well, you'll see when we get there.' He cracked a little smile and strode off ahead of me.

We headed into an alley off the main street and turned a few corners before coming to a bright red postbox. The cylindrical shape was already rare by that time, and I approached to give it a pat on the head.

'This way!'

I turned around at the sound of his voice to find him with a hand on a glass door.

'So you've been here before!' Takarada-san's eyes popped wide in surprise.

'Yes, but it was just that once, so I didn't remember where it was.'

'That makes sense . . .' He seemed deeply moved.

'The way you greeted me so politely, I almost felt like I'd

slipped back in time. I think he was probably a bit older than you are now, but in the sense of manner or, like, the way you carry yourself, you're just like him. He was so good to me.'

'I see . . .'

When we entered the shop, my grandfather said, 'Hi there!' as if he were close with the manager.

'Irasshaimase, Sahara-sama. You have a companion today, I see.'

'Indeed, I do. This is my grandson, Tomio. Say hello, Tomio. This is the manager, Kensui Takarada-san.'

'. . . Hello.' I was naturally shy, so that was all I could manage.

'Hello. Kensui Takarada, the manager of Shihodo Stationery, at your service. I hope you'll like the shop as much as your grandfather,' he greeted me politely. I'd never met a grown-up who greeted a kid with so much courtesy before, so I was really surprised. 'So, Sahara-sama, you're strolling Ginza with your grandson today? It's a weekday, so isn't it a school day?'

He asked bluntly, so the two must have known each other for a long time.

My grandfather had me take out my coloured pencils, and he began explaining the events of the previous day.

'I thought he was right. So I figured since I bought the pencils here, I would ask you to let the coloured pencil company know.'

Even as an elementary schooler, I felt like that was a pointless thing to say to the stationery shop manager, so he must have felt totally bewildered. But he didn't let any of it show, instead nodding emphatically.

'I see . . . You do have a point. I'll pass along the message.

Coloured Pencils

But since the colour names are industry custom, they may not change them right away.'

My grandfather nodded deeply and said, 'Well, yeah . . . But that's fine. I came because it won't hurt to tell them. I could have written a letter and sent it directly to the manufacturer or called customer service, but I thought the opinion might have more impact coming from a major retail client like Shihodo rather than as the lament of an ordinary citizen.'

'I'm not sure I move enough product to puff my chest out and say I'm a major client, but . . . it's true that we've been doing business with the pencil companies since their founding. So I'll start by contacting them through the salespeople Shihodo does business with.'

'Great, thank you.'

I thought it was a bit much, but at the same time, as a kid, the fact that my grandfather had gone out of his way to come to Ginza and make this request to the stationery shop did make me happy.

The manager was making a note when his hand suddenly stopped as he fell to thinking.

'As I said, I'll let them know, but I doubt anything will change right away. I do think Tomio-kun is right, though. I sold you these pencils, and I did the engraving. Since we're connected in that way, it's vexing to just wait around hoping.'

'Yeah. But, mm . . . It's not as if there's anything else we can do about it.'

The manager shook his head. 'Well, leave it to me. I have a bit of an idea. Please wait just a moment.' He ran into the back and returned carrying a basket with a few little containers inside. 'Apologies for the wait. Why don't we erase the names on the pencils and change them to names that feel right to Tomio-kun? We can use the engraving machine here at the shop to put in whatever words you like.'

'Ohhh, that never occurred to me,' my grandfather answered before turning to me. '*Hadairo*, chairo and mizuiro were the ones that bothered you, right?'

'Yeah.'

Upon my answer, the manager nodded firmly and took those three pencils out of the case. 'Then let's start with these three.'

With that, he picked up hadairo and used sandpaper to take the name off. Then he took the lid off a jar of what looked like plastic model paint and used a brush to put colour back onto the pencil's wood.

'There, now the word "hadairo" is gone. This is quick-drying paint, so it'll be dry by the time I've done the other two. While you wait, think about what you want to change the name to,' he prompted, offering me a notepad and pencil.

My grandfather and I looked at each other.

'. . . I wonder what I should call it.'

My grandfather appeared to be a bit stumped. 'Hmm. "Skin colour" is definitely weird, but as for what would be good to call it instead . . . That's a tough one.' He crossed his arms and cocked his head.

Just then, the manager offered us a hint as he shaved the writing off chairo and mizuiro. 'In English, "hadairo" is often called "pale orange" or "light orange".'

'I see. But using English just for colours is a bit . . . Tomio, what do you use this colour to draw?'

I didn't have a ready answer for the sudden question.

'Hmm . . . Maybe . . . *tarako?*'

Coloured Pencils

'Tarako? You sure are a weird one.' It must have been a really unexpected answer; the pitch of his voice rose a little. But at the time, I was always drawing my favourite foods, which included cod roe. 'Then "*tarakoiro*"? Doesn't really have a ring to it . . .'

'Maybe if we "grill them" and call it "*yakitarako*"?' I wrote it in the notepad.

'Ah, I see. That seems good!' He nodded emphatically and gave me a big smile.

Then the manager said, 'All right, I'll do the engraving now,' and began arranging the type.

'In those days, I think this was in a corner of the sales floor.' I lightly touched the machine. Back then, it had appeared larger and clunkier, but looking at it now, it seemed surprisingly small.

'My grandfather was the type of person who got anxious if he didn't keep things where he could see them . . . But though the machine does have a cover, it heats up and imparts a pretty strong force. I worried about what might happen if a small child got their hands on it, so I moved it to the basement.'

'I see . . . But, at any rate, your predecessor used this machine to engrave the new names on my coloured pencils.'

When I offered the yakitarako pencil to Takarada-san, he stroked it tenderly.

'After that, there was a movement to quit using the "skin colour" phrasing, so now many companies call it *usudaidaiiro* or "pale orange" in katakana.'

'I'm sure it's thanks to your predecessor reaching out to the coloured pencil companies.'

Notes from the Ginza Shihodo Stationery Shop

Takarada-san shook his head. 'Sadly, it didn't happen until around the year 2000, so I don't think he had any direct effect . . . But he was a very conscientious person, so I'm sure he did contact the pencil makers. But I think the change took way too long. More people should have been considering these things sooner.'

Then it was my turn to shake my head. 'No, there's no such thing as too late. As soon as you realise is enough.'

Takarada-san nodded and said, 'I feel like you just said to me the kind of thing I'm generally saying to my customers.'

'Well, that's because I'm older than you. You gotta let us older fellows look good now and then.'

He shook his head with a wry smile.

'That's one down. Now, what to do about chairo? Yesterday you were calling it mugichairo.'

I picked up the brown pencil. 'Yeah, this does look like the colour of barley tea.'

'Then how about we go with that? After all, these are your coloured pencils. Let's call them what you want to call them.'

My grandfather wrote 'mugichairo' on the notepad.

'Oh, before we just did "yakitarako" so maybe we don't need the "iro"? It could just be "mugicha".'

I crossed out the 'iro' he'd written.

'Ah, I see. Sure, why not?' He gave me a small but firm nod.

'Oh, that word includes a *dakuten* and a small *ya* . . . Mmm, ah, yes, I can do that. Now please decide what to do with mizuiro,' said the manager as he assembled the type for the new name.

Coloured Pencils

'Mizuiro . . . It's a light blue, so how about *usuao?*'

'But just diluting blue doesn't make it mizuiro. It's a colour right between blue and white.'

'True . . .' Hearing my assertion, my grandfather put a hand to his chin and mulled.

I was thinking about the idea of it being a colour 'right between blue and white'. As I thought it over, for some reason, a blue sky came to mind.

'Um . . . what about *sorairo?* I think it's pretty similar to the colour of the sky on a day with nice weather.'

'Ooh,' said Grandpa, crinkling his face into a smile. But he immediately had second thoughts and shook his head. 'You're right that mizuiro looks like the sky on a clear day. But some days have fair weather, and some don't – there's not just one "sky colour". Just like human skin colours. The sky might not be very happy to be stereotyped.'

My grandfather and I both fixed our eyes on the mizuiro pencil, almost like a staring contest.

Perhaps unable to simply stand by, the manager had an idea for us.

'How about this?' He picked up a pencil and wrote *nihonbare* in the notebook – a sunny sky without a single cloud.

'Ohhh . . .'

'Hmm, nihonbare, nihonbare, nihonbare . . . It's good! I like it!' I shouted in spite of myself.

'Great! Let's go with that. Feels auspicious somehow.' My grandfather nodded with a smile.

'Then that's what I'll do.'

He must have collected all the type before we knew it, because the work was done in a flash.

Notes from the Ginza Shihodo Stationery Shop

Thus, the three coloured pencils were given their new names: yakitarako, mugicha and nihonbare.

As my grandfather and I admired the newly engraved pencils, the manager began altering the tin.

He painted over the old names with steely grey paint and then used a fine brush to write the new names. He skilfully mimicked the typeface – so well that unless you looked closely, you couldn't tell the names had been rewritten.

After all the alterations were made, the time was coming up to three o'clock. We had arrived at Shihodo a little after one, which meant we had been being helped for nearly two hours. Strangely, during that whole time, not a single customer had entered the shop, and no one interrupted us.

'Thank you so much for your time and efforts. It's only a token of our gratitude, but please accept it.'

Grandpa presented a little envelope. The characters *matsu no ha* were printed on it, indicating a modest thank-you.

'Oh no, I can't accept this.'

'I bought the envelope here, so it looks very fancy, but don't worry. Inside is just a little tip.'

The manager accepted in a much-obliged way.

After seeing us outside, he stood next to the postbox, waving until we turned the corner.

'Hey, take me again sometime.'

'To Ginza? I guess you got a taste for melon soda floats, huh?'

'No, to that man's shop!'

'Oh? Sure, we can go, but how come?'

'I mean, he had so much drawing paper and paints and stuff. And expensive pens like grown-ups use. Next time, I want to spend a while checking everything out.'

Coloured Pencils

My grandfather had a big, happy smile on his face. 'OK, I promise we can come again together.'

'Yay!'

But the promise couldn't be kept.

*

'My grandfather died suddenly at the end of that year. He was only a couple years over sixty – an early death even considering the lower average life expectancy back then. But, as they say, "Ups and downs come woven together like a rope," and around the same time, my father returned from the US.'

'So after that, you lived in America?'

I nodded. 'We got rid of almost all our stuff. My mother took a single suitcase, and I took just a backpack. Despite throwing away nearly everything else, I kept my coloured pencils.'

Takarada-san lined the pencils up in the case and stroked the sticker on the inner cover. 'I felt like the engraving credit sticker was overly aggressive self-promotion, so I did away with it a long time ago, but hearing your story, I'd kind of like to bring it back.'

'Please do.'

When we returned to the ground floor, we found Ryoko asleep in the chair next to the till. It must have been awfully slow.

'Sheesh, talk about being off your guard,' Takarada-san grumbled.

'Can you make it with so few customers?' I asked bluntly.

Takarada-san emitted a little sigh. 'Well, just barely. It's only me, so we manage somehow. And there are a number of shops and offices in Ginza that we've been doing business with for ages. We deliver things to them, too.'

'Ohhh . . .'

Perhaps our voices had woken Ryoko. She stood up and

Notes from the Ginza Shihodo Stationery Shop

stretched. 'Oh, c'mon . . . Quit being so carefree and aim to prosper!'

Takarada-san and I exchanged a glance.

'Well, how about I contribute to your sales?'

I grabbed five sets each of the Uni Colored Pencil, Uni Water Color and Uni Arterase series.

Takarada-san hurried over with a shopping basket. 'But you don't have to do that for me!'

I shook my head. 'No, I want them. I need souvenirs for my family, friends and co-workers at the studio. I'd also like one of those pencil sharpeners, too.'

'Oh, then how about these? They're brush pens, but they come in a huge variety of colours.' Ryoko invited me deeper into the shop.

'Oh, I'll explain. Uhhh, this is the ZIG Clean Color FB series from Kuretake. The soft brush hairs are good for colouring. There are twelve basic colours that come in four different intensities for a total of forty-eight. You can use a blender or water brush to create gradations and mix colours. There are also these ZIG Memory System Wink of Luna brushes with colours that stand out even on dark paper.'

'They all look great.'

I tossed product after product into the basket, and it was full in the blink of an eye.

* * *

It was still drizzling. The long rainy spells of autumn were practically the natural nemesis of Ginza with its lack of covered arcades. Having exited the glass double doors to observe the weather, Ken Takarada, the manager of Shihodo Stationery,

Coloured Pencils

emitted a short sigh. He shook his head and was about to go back inside the shop.

Just then, he noticed a woman with a red umbrella approaching with quick steps. She wore a trench coat and a wine-red beret and was carrying a paper bag. In her other hand was her phone, and she repeatedly glanced around – perhaps comparing the map on her app to her surroundings.

Then she seemed to suddenly notice the old, cylindrical postbox, and upon approaching it, she turned towards Shihodo.

When Ken bobbed his head to her, she jogged up the steps outside.

'Umm, is this Shihodo? The stationery shop?'

She'd rushed up to him so suddenly, he nearly lost his nerve. 'Y-yes, it is. This is Shihodo.'

'Ohhh, good. I have something for you.' She held out the paper bag.

'We don't need to stand around out here. Why don't you come inside?'

The woman hesitated for a moment, but she shook her head as if to convince herself. 'No, I'd love to, but I need to get right back.'

Ken accepted the paper bag. The item inside was securely wrapped with packing materials, so he couldn't tell what it was.

In response to his dubious expression, she added, 'I think it's a picture,' and pulled an envelope out of her pocket. 'I was told to give you this along with it.'

The envelope said *Takarada-sama* on the front, and the sender was listed as Tommy Davis.

'Umm . . . what exactly . . .?'

Notes from the Ginza Shihodo Stationery Shop

'I'm the interpreter who works with Tommy-san when he's in Japan. A bunch of stuff arrived in preparation for his next job, and this was in among those packages.'

'I see...'

Ken nodded, and the woman excused herself with a, 'Well, I'd be off, then.'

After seeing her off with a bow, Ken went back inside. He immediately took a box cutter out of the drawer at the counter and opened the envelope and unwrapped the package.

Inside the bag was a framed picture featuring the willow-lined street; the red, cylindrical postbox; and Shihodo.

'Wow...' he couldn't help but murmur. Then he looked inside the envelope to find a letter.

Dear Takarada-san,

> *I'm so grateful for all your assistance when I visited. Getting the chance to take my time at the Shihodo of my memories was an opportunity I wouldn't trade for anything. Thank you so much.*
>
> *I made all sorts of burdensome requests, yet you handled each one so courteously. Now I've been taken care of so well by two generations of managers; I don't know how to thank you enough.*
>
> *So as a token of my gratitude, I decided to try drawing Shihodo with my coloured pencils. I don't know if it will be to your taste, but I hope you'll accept it.*
>
> *Also, the meetings about the new show – why I went to Japan in the first place – finished up without a hitch and now we've proceeded to constructing the main set. We*

should have our first performance during Golden Week next year. I'd be delighted if you and Ryoko-san would come see it. I'll be in Japan for the opening, so I'd like to stop by Shihodo again.

Tomio

After reading the letter, Ken returned it to the envelope, pressed his palms together as if in prayer and looked to the heavens. 'Thank you.'

In one corner of Ginza, Tokyo – Shihodo Stationery. The drizzle seemed liable to continue, but the shop was enveloped in a peaceful, warm atmosphere.